THE MAIN OFFICE

To Linda,
Welcome to the pages
of this book. Step inside and
live each story with me!
I hope you love every minute —

Crystal

Crystal Lee

PAGE PUBLISHING, INC.
New York, NY

First originally published by Page Publishing, Inc. 2018

ISBN 978-1-64298-850-5 (Paperback)
ISBN 978-1-64298-851-2 (Digital)

Printed in the United States of America

Dedicated to my children and to my husband who had to put up with attending the school where their mom worked and who had to listen to all of these stories at dinnertime throughout the years. I love you, and I hope you always remember the good times in school.

CONTENTS

Introduction 7

Part One: May the Technological Force Be with You 11

Chapter 1: Africa Is Calling 13
Chapter 2: When Good Machines Go Bad 21
Chapter 3: Guys Who Get Pocket Protectors for Christmas 31
Chapter 4: Now, for Your Viewing Pleasure 37

Part Two: People Who Need People Are the Luckiest People 47

Chapter 5: Mr. Smith Goes to Middle School 49
Chapter 6: Creative Alphabetizing 58
Chapter 7: There's No Substitute for a Good Substitute 65
Chapter 8: Too School for Cool 75
Chapter 9: Go Sell Crazy Somewhere Else 83

Part Three: Animals at Large 95

Chapter 10: Beverly with the Friendly Eyes 97
Chapter 11: Monty the Python 105
Chapter 12: Everyone and Their Dogs 111
Chapter 13: Life Is Better with a Smart Dog 118

Part Four: Are You Going to Eat That? 129

Chapter 14: All the Gum and Nothing but the Gum 131

Chapter 15: For Pete's Sake 142

Chapter 16: School Lunch Dismissed..149

Chapter 17: Save the Cheese Burgers in Paradise.......................157

Part Five: In the End 167

Chapter 18: The Wheels on the Bus Go Round and Round.......169

Chapter 19: The Best-Laid Plans..179

Chapter 20: Oh, Holiday Bush . . . Oh, Holiday Bush...............188

Chapter 21: A House Fell on Her Sister 197

Chapter 22: The Final Days 206

INTRODUCTION

Not many people can remember the first time they set foot in a school, the first day of kindergarten, for most is a blur that their mom always talks about with a melancholy smile on her face and maybe a tear because they're all grown up now, but they have no recollection of at all.

I was no different. I don't have a clue what my first day of kindergarten was like. I can barely remember the schoolhouse itself because it isn't even standing anymore. My first clear memory of school was the first day of fourth grade. I remember it because during the summer between third and fourth grade, I got glasses. I was so excited to show them to my classmates and my teacher, Mrs. Reed, a large woman who smelled kind of funny, and I was naive enough to think *they* were going to be excited as well.

As you can imagine, excitement was not their first reaction. My teacher tried to feign enthusiasm, though she knew what would be in store for me with my classmates. The kids were merciless with their teasing and jokes, and when I got my school pictures that fall, I cried for three days. However, I didn't perish from embarrassment. I survived as most children who get glasses in grade school do, and life went on.

Junior high came and went and was filled with memories of being the only seventh grader to make the school choir and earn a part in the school play, then passing out on stage during the performance. Again, I survived, just, and stumbled my way to high school where I was a bit lost. Not in a popular group or a club member, I floated my way through with one or two close friends with the same fortune. We didn't attend proms, we hung out with the girls' sports teams even though we didn't play, and we earned good grades. We kept to ourselves, enjoyed our adolescence, and we muddled along until graduation.

College was a bit easier socially. The first college I attended was a small campus with a few old buildings that were on the city's historic list, and I thrived in the tight-knit community. Because they didn't offer the degree I was seeking, I transferred after two years to a larger university to study food and nutrition. My father wanted me to be involved in the medical arts so I could meet and marry the doctor of his dreams. So I worked and studied and, for the most part, got As and Bs, and no one was more surprised than me when I actually graduated. I was the first in my family to do so, and my mother was very proud. My father had passed a year earlier, and he never saw me receive my diploma.

How was I going to use my degree? That was the next big question. I had worked in a hospital, a department store, and was part of an office cleaning staff, all at the same time while I was attending college to avoid student loans. Most of the class I had graduated with would be going on to be registered dieticians, but I'd had my fill of hospital food and bureaucracy, so I chose a different route.

I wanted to open a bed and breakfast and a small catering business. Instead, I married and engineer and had a family. Two sons, whom I was lucky enough to stay at home with and raise myself. Four years of college was really paying off so far.

After my youngest son started school, I'd spent enough time at home, and I decided it was time to go back to work. I was leafing through a newsletter from the elementary school when I saw a notice for a part-time library aide that was needed at the high school just around the corner from our home.

That's the perfect job! I thought, and I was launched once again back into the public education system, this time on the other side of the counter.

I worked my way up from part-time library aide to secretary to the principal, and I loved every minute of my career. After eighteen years, I have stories for just about every occasion and dirt on just about everyone I worked with. I have had some rare encounters and some gems that I will never forget.

People would ask me what I did for a living, and I'd tell them that I'd been a secretary in the main office in the public-school system for the better part of eighteen years. Then they'd say things like, "I bet you've seen it all," or "I guess you have a lot of stories you could tell."

I would relate some of my better tales, and then they'd say, "You should write a book about that."

I had always kept a small journal of my main office days. I wrote about the funniest, weirdest, or wildest and most unusual events that happened during my years, from when I started as a library assistant to when I retired as a principal's secretary, that I could remember.

When I finally reread what I'd written in my diary I thought, *Erma Bombeck, I not, but I might be able to put together a few sentences and paragraphs that people may want to read and that might make them laugh.*

So I finally did. I wrote this book, and as I did, I relived every experience and each day. I stretched the truth a bit and changed the names to protect the semi-innocent and loved every minute of it.

I wanted to write a book about a job that was all at once exhilarating, purposeful, rewarding, frustrating, and as funny as real life can be. A book full of stories that were all inspired by events that actually happened but that were too fantastical to be believed.

I wanted to write a book that nearly everyone could relate to. A book that was G-rated, that every age group could read and nod because they'd know exactly how that felt.

One of the most poignant questions I was ever asked by a teacher is one that I still remember today. She asked the class, "If everyone in the world looked the same, what would make you stand out?"

In other words, how would we know you if we all looked alike? Then we were asked to write a thousand-word essay about our answer. I thought about that question quite a bit as I wrote, because as you read a book, any book you might not know exactly what the author looked like, but you might be able to know who the author is by the style of the writing or maybe other books they have written.

The answer to that question for me was that I would hope people would know me by my compassion, my willingness to help others, and the use of wit to keep others calm in a tense or anxious situation—usually good-natured and even-tempered. These have greatly influenced me in my career choice and have served me well through my years in the public-school system.

If you are a teacher, a student, or the parent of a student, hopefully you will find this book enjoyable and enlightening. I hope it takes you back to your school days and your experiences with public education, and I hope it makes you smile with delight.

Hopefully, you will be able to relate to some or all of them in one way or another. I feel optimistic that you will find a connection with a few of the characters that follow and you will be transported back to your school days or your child's school days, and these stories will invoke a chuckle. You might even encounter some surprises along the way and perhaps learns a lesson or two.

Enjoy!

PART ONE

MAY THE TECHNOLOGICAL FORCE BE WITH YOU

CHAPTER 1

AFRICA IS CALLING

"Hurray!" I exclaimed as I ripped the red Santa-clad paper off the box, removed the lid and ogled the brand-new, shiny smartphone my family had given me for Christmas. My husband was so excited, and my two sons even more so. They were finally bringing me into the technology-saturated twenty-first century.

Now I could check my grocery list on my phone notes while walking down the aisles of the grocery store, I could text my neighbor who was standing on queue just two lines down in the same store, and I could listen to music with earphones while the clerk was trying to ask me a question. I could do just about everything on this device even make a simple call.

At first, I resisted, insisting that I didn't need a cell phone, let alone a smart one, nor did I need to be accessible 24/7 to all of my friends, family, and acquaintances. They assured me that I would love it, and I'd be on Facebook in no time.

Not Facebook! I thought to myself.

The last thing I needed was the headache of keeping track of all my friends going for a walk, taking their kids on vacation, or putting all of their drama out there for everyone to share with them. I didn't need theirs; I had my own, and I certainly didn't want to share it with everyone or anyone for that matter. I didn't need a phone to message me every time one of them took an aspirin.

Nor did I need a phone to keep track of my FUN (frequently used numbers); I could already remember my families' phone numbers without my phone book or speed dial. Gradually though, my phone grew on me, and I warmed up to it. Not to the extent of my children and friends; I did not sleep with it under my pillow or handcuff it to my wrist. I secretly hoped they would never find out that a phone just couldn't be that important.

I texted in complete sentences which made my children laugh at me, and I did not know what an emoji was for the longest time. Even if I did know I wouldn't know where to locate one. I could not text sixty words per minute, but I did okay, and I learned to use most of the accessories that accompanied it. It took only a few months to learn how to unlock my screen; after that it was all downhill.

In the year 2015, when I received my phone, 68 percent of Americans owned a smartphone. I would have guessed a higher number, but it must be right because the internet doesn't lie. Research (on the internet) also shows that 88 percent of teens in the US thirteen to seventeen years of age have a cell phone. No big surprise there.

Of those, 90 percent text every day. In fact, the average teen in that age group receives or sends thirty texts per day, *not* including Facebook, Instagram, Twitter, and many other social media posts. Ninety-one percent of teens access the internet from their phones (this is where they learn that if it's on the internet, it's true). No wonder they don't get much schoolwork done.

I have heard stories about schools or, more to the point, teachers who allow students to not only have access to their cell phones in class but also put them to use, solving math problems, writing papers, or doing research. I always find myself wondering how those teachers monitor students, to keep them from posting on Facebook, texting friends in other classes, or just playing around catching a wave and surfing the net.

The majority of schools in the district which was my employer had a no-phones policy. Some administrators might emplace a policy that students could have them in their backpacks but the phones themselves be turned off.

Our school always wanted a no-cell-phones-in-class-period policy in our educational fairytale world. However, in reality, we knew this would never fly. So we stressed leaving cell phones in lockers and not having them accessible at all. Which also would probably never fly, but we had to try something.

The most common objection to this policy was, believe it or not, from the parents.

"What happens if I need to reach my student?" they would ask.

Travel way back in time with me now, you know, back before everyone and their pet monkey had a cell phone, and remember when all you had to do to get a message to your student was to call the main office. The all-too-efficient office staff would locate the student in question, call them down to the main office, where they would then return Mom's call. This method worked for centuries in public schools. But since the advent of instant communication, if a parent couldn't call and immediately hear their child's voice, panic ensued.

I have actually had parents call the office and ask for a specific teacher's room, telling me they were that teacher's relative, and after they were connected, they would ask to speak to their student. Are you kidding me?

One of our mama bears who came to the school several times a week always began the conversation this way: "I am Mrs. Ashby, Melissa Ashby's mom. All of my children have gone to school here."

She would state this like it was supposed to mean that she was entitled to special treatment or she should automatically move to the proverbial front of the line or head of the class BAE (before anyone else), yet this is how the dialogue began each time she entered the office.

However, it was different on this Tuesday. On this day, she marched up to my desk and announced that she had to check her daughter out of school because she was ill. Already knowing the answer, I still had to ask, "How do you know she is sick?" I asked in what I hoped wasn't an accusatory tone.

"She is in the bathroom throwing up her breakfast, and she texted me."

Of course, she did! I thought as I sat at my desk, looking like a total idiot because I didn't know anything about any student being ill, let alone *her* daughter.

Now I had to explain to *her* that I had no way of knowing that her daughter was sick or where her daughter even was, because she could have been in one of a dozen bathrooms in the school, texting Mom and apparently throwing up at the same time.

Upon further investigation, the teacher didn't know she was sick either, because all Melissa had said was that she needed to visit the restroom. I didn't know she was ill because the procedure would be for her to come to the restroom in the office where we could help her and then call her mom. See what happens when you don't follow procedure? The whole system fails!!

Evidently, Melissa was too sick to come to the office to call home, but not too sick to text while throwing up in the restroom. A search party was sent out to find her, and after she was found safe and sound, tears were shed, and the sickly child was released on her own recognizance to her mother's care—the ordeal was over. There were checks and balances for these life-and-death situations, but cell phones have thrown all the processes out the window and tossed them like Dorothy in a Kansas tornado.

Keeping teenagers off their cell phones was like trying to keep Donald Trump off his Twitter account and inciting riots during his presidential campaign. It just wasn't going to happen. His smart-phone was like a pacifier was to a baby, except he can start a war with his. Our students were connected to their phones like they were lifelines. They had to have them in their hand every waking moment just in case a fight broke out between two girls and you just had to share it on Instagram. Phones were vital, class or no class.

Our recourse for having cell phones in class was this: If you are caught with your cell phone out in class, no matter what the reason, your phone will be confiscated for the day. The second time you are caught, your phone will be confiscated for twenty-four hours, and your parent will be required to pick it up.

Parents can be different animals. They come in all shapes and sizes. They can be protective mama bears or inattentive rabbits who leave their babes after a couple of weeks to fend for themselves. One thing is for sure—they all act differently in different situations.

When picking up a child's cell phone that has been confiscated, there are two basic groups of parents. Group one is embarrassed because their child has no accountability whatsoever and now they have to come to pick up the incarcerated phone and feel guilty that they let their child have a phone at all without the capacity for holding them responsible. They go on about how they are going to take the phone away (when we all know they won't) and how they will ground the student until college (and we all know that's a lot of hot air), and they swear it will never happen again, which it always does.

The second group is worried about their time, letting you know that it is absolutely unacceptable that they had to come all the way to school just to pick up a phone—I mean WTBDA (what's the big deal anyway)?

This group does not even attempt to pretend that they will withhold the phone or have a talk with their student. They take the phone from your hand, roll their eyes at you, and in most cases, they make sure you are still watching as they make a big show of giving the phone back to the student. Headdesk! (This is the equivalent of banging your head on the desk in cyberspeak or teenese, the language of the middle school cyber world.)

We were smart enough in the main office to only make phones available at the end of the school day so that the students wouldn't just return to class and use it again and have it confiscated more than once in a day. However, occasionally, we were surprised by a parent who said, "I have no backbone, and I would appreciate it if you could just hold on to this thing for a week or two so I won't be tempted to give it back."

We would be glad to help you out with that.

There were so many times, however, that the parents were actually the problem. They would be the culprit on the other end of the cell phone, texting their child, SMH (shaking my head).

During registration, way before the first day of school, parents are given a written statement of cell phone rules so that they can take it home, fix it to their fridges with magnets, and promptly ignore it.

They know, for example, that the second time their child is caught with a cell phone out in class, they, as the parent, will be required to come in person and pick it up. They can't just call in and ask us to give it back to their student; still they try. They will call and give you every excuse imaginable . . . Now we know where the kids get it. One parent whose child was from South Africa called and said, "My son must have his phone returned to him." He was very insistent.

Since they transferred in late in the school year, it was entirely possible that they did not know the rule or hadn't had it explained to them. So I let him know that this was the second time the phone had been confiscated because his son had been using it and he would have to come into the school to retrieve it.

It is truly amazing how often the parent never knows about the first time. Somehow the child always seems to forget to mention that. So this particular parent became very angry with me when I informed him that his son would not be allowed to have his phone. He gave me a host of excuses that included his mother needed to text him (not the most persuasive argument for my returning his phone).

Then he said that the family needed to be in constant communication; he wouldn't elaborate on why. Then he tried the I-am-going-to-get-a lawyer-and-sue-you approach, which many parents before him had tried and failed with. He threatened to call the police because we had stolen personal property, another tactic that had been tried—many times, in fact.

Finally, he was so frustrated by my calm response to every opposition, he yelled through the phone and into my ear, "But Africa is calling!"

I must admit that that was a new one for me. I had not heard that before, and it CMOG (caught me off guard). Yes, it would seem that the family was expecting an important call from Africa, and this was their only phone. To which I suggested that, if that were the case, maybe he should pick up the phone and keep it with him or the boy's mother so that *they* could indeed receive the important call and not their twelve-year-old son. The man hung up on me, apparently not satisfied with my answer to his exclamation.

At the end of the day, the boy's mother came in and picked up the cell phone and apologized for her husband's rudeness and promised the incident would not be repeated. To my knowledge, it never was, thank goodness for mothers and their levelheadedness.

Teenagers will use any—and I do mean *any*—reason to be on their phone. The students who aren't quite A students will use the standard "It fell out of my backpack, and I was just picking it up when it happened to go off." Never mind that the pack was upright and zipped . . . Hey, it could happen.

They always get caught too. They think they are sly and don't realize that if you are looking in your lap for the entire class time, it's a good bet the teacher knows you have a cell phone. Even while they are texting, they have little codes like PAW (parents are watching) and TAW (teachers are watching) that should alert their conspirators to the fact that they are about to have their smartphone confiscated by a smarter teacher.

Then there are the students who fall back on the oldie but goodie "I was only checking the time." Never mind that there is a clock in every room in the building. What's sad about this excuse is that with the technology boom, many teenagers in the twenty-first century cannot tell time on a traditional clock with hands and numbers. They have grown up in the digital era, and they have never been taught to tell time. If the numbers don't flash across the screen, giving them the instant information they crave and demand, they are lost.

They don't know how to find out what the time is without their phones, making world-famous clocks like Big Ben on Elizabeth Tower in London's palace of Westminster *just* a landmark for sightseers instead of a timepiece for all of London. Makkahs Royal Clock in Mecca, Saudi Arabia, the clock with the largest face in the world, a record 141-feet in diameter, now becomes useless to the teenagers of the world. And the clock erected in Moscow, Russia's Red Square in 1625 is now obsolete.

How on earth would Marty McFly, the young hero in *Back to the Future*, save the day if he couldn't tell the time on the Hill Valley Clock Tower? He would have missed the lightning strike at 10:04 p.m. that sent him *back to the future*. So our youth today would be in a world of hurt if they had to tell time on a traditional clock to save them in some way. Unbelievable, IMO (in my opinion).

Then, there are the selfies—Lord have mercy, the selfies. There are teenagers that think that they are the cutest things ever to walk the planet, and they think that everyone should have every possible chance to see them. So let the selfies begin!

If you have ever sat quietly in a crowded place like a mall or a movie theatre between shows and watched the people, you will see thousands of pics (pictures) being taken and instantly uploaded and posted on some social media site. Because everyone should know when you are at the mall and who you went to the movies with.

The faces they make! Teenagers are all about the silly faces. Basically, how stupid can they be? Yeah, let's share *that* with everyone we know. Twenty-somethings are all about how beautiful and cool they are. They fix their hair, make sexy kissy faces, and share with all the people of the opposite sex that they know.

The younger crowd wants all their friends in all their pics, so they all act crazy together. The older crowd—I'm talking about eighteen-to-twenty-five-year-old group now—want only themselves in their pics. No one will want to see anyone but them anyway. Right?

They all act like they are models in the making, but it doesn't matter how many selfies you take and post; it still doesn't make you the next Christy Brinkley or Cindy Crawford. WTD (what's the deal)?

The experts agree that the selfie syndrome is a means of self-representation for these selfie masters, especially girls. They mimic the latest celeb who posts every pic and detail of herself online; the teenage girls then post their selfies and details and wait for the 'likes' to roll in.

They take hundreds of pics of themselves for validation and post them for external assurance of how popular, important, and beautiful they are. In theory—and let's just admit it—it's fun!

What's really fun is anticipating what is up and coming for the next generation of cyber princesses. Video cameras in iPhones that are specifically geared to post videos on social media? Hold on to your tiaras!

All the cyber slang used in this chapter was provided by makeuseof.com, noslang.com, and my technologically advanced sons. Check it out ICYMI (in case you missed it).

CHAPTER 2

WHEN GOOD MACHINES
GO BAD

I started working for the school district just as my youngest son
started kindergarten. I was hired on as a part-time library aide
at the high school right around the corner from our home. It was,
hands down, the best job I ever had. The library was not an incredi-
bly busy place, and the kids that were there were the kids that wanted
to be there, so there were very few disruptions or behavior issues.

When I first started there, we actually still had the card catalog.
Students today don't even know what the blazes a card catalog was
or did, but it would be a few more years yet until everything was
available on the computer and the index cards would become recycle
fodder. Our library was quiet and full of books, just like a library
should be, and I never wanted to leave.

I never really *had* to leave. My workday was filled with pushing
a cart with book to reshelf, finding books for research and reading
books when time permitted. So consequently, nobody in the school
really knew who I was or that I was even there. Once a day, I would
sneak from the library through a side door and hurry down a short
hallway to the mail room, where I would collect my mail and then
scurry back to the sanctuary that was my office cubicle in the library
like a mouse with a crumb.

One year the administration asked for volunteers from all over
the school to help with registration, and I decided to venture outside

the library and lend my mad reading and book-shelving skills to the registration process. Turns out I was not too bad away from my sub-dued library. I loved to meet the teachers and other staff members who kept the school running, and I liked working with the students and their parents. I could get used to life on the outside in the hub-bub of the school.

I helped one particular mom who was totally lost in the reg-istration process and ended up at the payment station before she'd even met with a counselor or any of the other twenty-three things she needed to do before she paid the fees. I left my station for a few min-utes to walk her back to the front and helped her maneuver through the lines, forms, and red tape. She was so grateful that she wrote a nice thank-you note the principal on my behalf.

It wasn't long afterward that the principal called me to his office. I fixed my hair, checked to make sure I didn't have anything in my teeth, and trudged toward the main office. Just like a student, I wondered during the journey, "Was I in trouble?" "Why did he want to see me?" "Should I start looking for another job?" working myself into a panic. When I arrived, he showed me the letter and asked if I would like to become a member of the youth advocate team for freshmen and sophomores. I decided to venture out among the masses to join forces with the people actually changing the lives of the kids. I worked as a sort of liaison between the underclassmen and high-risk students and the faculty. As such, I didn't have much spare time to read, but I did see a lot more students, which pleased me.

I had only been there a short time when I was asked to change positions again. I was on to the main office where things really got crazy. I thought I had arrived. The main office was like Disneyland. It had all the lines, all the cartoon characters, and all the chaos of the main street of the famed amusement park. All that was missing was the electric light parade. It was high traffic and an even higher stress level. Parent complaints, teachers with problems to fix, and confused students filled my days. Boy, that library sure was looking good.

After a couple of years in Disneyland—I mean the main office—I landed at the office of the principal, every schoolboy's nightmare and secretary's dream. Secretary to the principal was the highest secretarial position you could hold at a school level. The secretarial staff, me included, looked upon the principal's secretary with awe. She was so smart, so put together, so organized. Once there, I quickly learned all that was a carefully manicured facade.

My first day as principal's secretary, I was sort of flying by the seat of my pants or, more aptly, the hem of my skirt. Turns out when you are the principal's secretary, everyone, including the principal, expects you to know everything. I was holding my own and treading water, then I ran into the postage machine. I wasn't afraid, at first. I mean how hard could it be? Anyway, I was the principal's secretary. Surely, this small piece of office equipment was no match for me.

It had a small inconspicuous scale where you weighed your letter before adding postage to it. It had a slot where you inserted your letter for just the right funds to be printed on it to get it delivered where you wanted it to go. It had a small screen where messages would appear to "help" me. I walked bravely up to it and weighed my letter—so far, so good. Then the innocent-looking apparatus asked me a question: "Ink is low, would you like to install new ink cartridge?"

Oh no. Yes, I think, so I depressed the button which answered in the affirmative. Then the instructions began fast and furious, I could hardly keep up. "Remove ink cartridge." While I was trying to figure out *how* to remove the ink cartridge, the machine asked, "Ink cartridge removed?"

"No, not yet," I spoke to the machine.

Okay, push this button, pull that handle, turn this dial, wiggle that door, and the used cartridge sprang free. Success! "Do you want to install new cartridge?" it asked. Well, yes, since I just successfully removed the old one, I will need to put in a new one, I think.

"Wait," it instructed. So I did. I waited and waited, then I waited some more. "Install cartridge," it ordered. So I turned the new cartridge this way and that until it looked like the piece fit the machinery puzzle, then I carefully clicked the new one into place.

"Preparing cartridge. Please wait." So I waited again. After a few minutes, it said, "Pretesting cartridge. Please wait." So I waited longer. "Configuring cartridge." All right already! "Test cartridge," the machine coaxed. I placed a blank envelope in the slot, and sure enough the ink worked. "Test placement," it urged. I inserted another blank envelope, and a complex line configuration showed up in the upper right corner. Okay, a successful test.

"Yes!" I whispered enthusiastically with a triumphant fist pump. "Test okay?" it asked.

"Affirmative," I said as I pushed the Yes button, wondering at the sanity of a woman who was carrying on a conversation with her postage machine that was probably smarter than she was.

I was instructed to *insert envelope*. What it should have said was insert *another* envelope. Apparently, the ink was ready, and I was cleared for take-off. I inserted the letter I wanted to mail. "Printing," the machine responded. "Please wait." I was becoming pretty good at waiting. "Remove envelope." The task was finally accomplished. I yanked the letter from the jaws of the postage machine and dropped it into the mail basket. Twenty minutes and a few less envelopes later, I had postage on my letter. The rest of the day should be a breeze.

Technology is essential in making an office, any office, run smoothly. I liken it to the force in the Star Wars saga. Nobody knows exactly what it is or how it works, but it flows through us and around us at all times, and it guides our entire office existence in one way or another. If there is no order in the technological force, there is no peace in the galaxy or in the main office.

A tremor in the technological force always begins with something small and innocent. A tiny flashing light or the absence of a tiny light, something that usually goes unnoticed or is ignored, but once the shudder in the force is felt and the ripples begin to spread, it can be a galactic catastrophe.

One such innocent shudder was an unremarkable message on our fax machine that read "Toner low." No big deal, you think. You might even make a mental note to change the toner and order a new one for the storage room, but it can wait, right? Sure, it can wait. You might even take notice of a second warning if you're not too busy. Hey, Ms. Secretary, this is your second warning: "Replace toner." But still, it isn't *that* serious, is it? These things are meant to give you a grace period, at least a few days. I mean it's only Tuesday. Surely, I will get to it by Wednesday or Thursday this week. I have plenty of time.

Then the normal everyday office stuff happens. The phones ring a few thousand times, several gym kids need Band-Aids for miscellaneous scrapes and injuries, a sick student throws up on the office carpet, three fights break out (one of those was between two PTA moms), and that was just one afternoon. After three days of distractions, I had forgotten all about the tiny little "low toner" message from our fax machine.

On Friday, I needed to call another school to request immunization records on a new student that was transferring to us.

"Just fax them over," I said, lightly, full of confidence and trust that our wonderful facsimile machine would deliver as it always had. I gave the number and asked the registrar to send over her documents.

Apparently, no one had noticed that we hadn't been receiving any faxes over the past couple of days. Of course, we had sent a few facsimiles, but our basket for received faxes was, in fact, empty.

How can that possibly be? We all wondered in a we-are-not-really-worried-but-something-must-be-terribly-wrong sort of way. Then I noticed the message in the small, inconspicuous box on the front of the machine:

"REPLACE TONER NOW!" it shouted at us. What it should have said was "I HAVE BEEN TELLING YOU GUYS FOR DAYS THAT THE TONER WAS LOW, SO STOP IGNORING ME AND FILL ME UP!"

Maybe that would have gotten our attention. So now we had a problem, a tremor in the technological force. Information had stopped moving, and the office had stopped running. What to do now? Well, first of all, don't panic! We can fix this. We have the technology.

What we didn't have was an extra toner. No, wait! I *had* ordered a replacement toner when I had received the first of many warnings. See? I am good for something.

I would find the box with the new toner cartridge, and the fax would begin working again. Got ya! However, the fax machine did not just magically begin working. There were other steps that had to be completed, and completed correctly, before the blasted machine—I mean the *blessed* machine—could resume functioning.

I dutifully read all the instructions. I gently took out the old toner cartridge, being ever so careful not to spill black charcoal dust all down the front of my outfit. I carefully turned the new cartridge this way and that until it would slip into the compartment where it was directed to go. I snapped it in.

Everyone in the office stood watching. We all gathered around the machine and gazed down upon it like it was a sick friend who might not recover. We watched and hoped, and I am sure that a few of us actually prayed that it would recover successfully and begin accepting faxes again.

"I am one with the force. The force is one with me," I chanted in my brain.

A minute went by, then two. All we needed to make the scene complete was suspenseful background music to heighten the anticipation of the moment.

"Just give it a moment," I said breathlessly, wondering what my next move would be if I could not revive the machine.

Would I have to perform CPR? Electric shock? Would I need a defibrillator? How do you give a fax machine mouth-to-mouth resuscitation? I wondered. A real Jedi would know what to do.

"Come on, baby . . . breathe," I coaxed, like an ER doctor about to lose a patient, willing him to live with the theatrical score building to a dramatic climax in the action.

"You can do it," came a voice from behind me.

Melodrama had gripped the entire office; the music was reaching its crescendo.

Finally, after what seemed like a lifetime, a little green light on the bottom of the screen flickered. Across the small screen the message read, "Toner replenishment in progress." A few minutes later, the machinery began to hum, and the apparatus coughed and chocked to life. Handshakes and high-fives all around. I felt like I had saved a life and done a heroic deed. Indeed, the office buzzed over the accomplishment. I sheathed my lightsaber like a bona-fide Jedi and turned to go back to work.

Then it started, the outpouring of paper. Documents that had been lost in the fax abyss were now found to be freed, printed, and read. A never-ending stream of documents commenced, gushing from the slot. Pages and pages surged as the machine worked overtime to keep up with the demand that was being placed on it. I began thinking that we might have to replace the toner again because of the number of documents being printed.

We had to put more paper in the tray to accommodate all that was being used. I silently mourned for all the trees in the forest. Then, quiet. A hush fell over the office. The printing of the documents was complete, and the machine rested. The entire office collectively breathed a sigh of relief and the flow in the technological force was restored. A catastrophe had been averted, the office was spared, and all was well until . . . a more serious tremor in the force occurred, and the galaxy trembled again.

I flipped on my computer one Monday morning, and *bam!* I got the ERROR message like a sucker punch to the gut. The message no one wants to see at any time, but usually pops up at the worst possible time. Apparently, my computer was now misbehaving, and I would have to reboot, restore, revive, and regenerate everything so that I could resume working. It is important to note that this was Monday. They always know, these machines that we depend on so much. They are quite like us; they are slow on Monday mornings and can't wait to stop working on Friday afternoons. The reboot usually took anywhere from twenty-five minutes to hours on end. So I flipped off my computer, literally and figuratively, and began anew. I felt like kicking the machine, but instead, I restarted it, and luckily, the apparatus fired up with no error message, and no further problems *that* day.

"I love technology," I said aloud, my voice thick with sarcasm. "It is such a wonderful thing."

And indeed it is, as long as it is functioning properly. But when wires, hard drives, and software of good machines behave badly, technology can be a frustrating challenge, and you may feel as though you are the only Jedi fighting the dark side of the force. Trust me, you are not. We are all fighting the good fight and winning, I think.

There are many business machines in every type of office, whether they be attorney's offices, doctor's offices, private investigation offices, or school offices. Everything from the most complicated calculator to a simple electric pencil sharpener is commonly used and mostly taken for granted. Computers, phones, faxes, printers, scanners, laminators, binders, and the most important of all, the copier.

The duplicator, or Xerox machine, as it became universally known, is found in *every* office across the country and all over the world. The minute the newly manufactured commercial Xerox machines came rolling off the assembly line in 1959, business offices were forever changed. At that time, because of the distinct need for the copy machine, manufacturers could hardly keep up with the demand.

Gone were the days of typing on a manual typewriter with a sheet of black carbon between the white pages to make a single copy. These machines could make copies at a clip of seven per minute. Today's Xerox machines can make sixty-five copies per minute, sort, stack, collate, staple, fold, punch holes, and make cappuccino frappes.

Historian Lynn Peril deemed the new-fangled machines fabulously liberating. The only real drawback they had was that the first of these reproductive miracles were prone to spontaneous combustion. Perfect for office use with all that paper around! Aside from that, they were truly a godsend for secretaries and for teachers.

I am witness that business will grind to a halt in a school if there is no copy machine. I don't know how schools ever operated without them back in the day when kitchen appliances came with power cords that weren't purchased separately, you had to know how to parallel park because your car wouldn't do it for you, and Bruce Jenner was still a guy.

Thousands upon thousands of copies run through a school copier every day. I have literally seen a line outside our copy room that would rival Disneyland's most popular ride with teachers craning their necks to see how much longer it would be until it was their turn.

Without the office copier, teachers would simply have to stop teaching, and students would simply have to stop learning. Today, if we still had one-room schoolhouses, that room would definitely have to be a copy room.

The most dreadful feeling that can happen in an office is when the copier stops working. Well, maybe the worst thing that could happen is the toilet could stop working; after that is the copier. Even the most experienced Jedi in the galaxy becomes helpless and all of them feel the turbulence in the force if the copier is amiss. There will be a multitude of competent, educated office personnel pushing buttons, pulling papers, tuning rollers, jiggling power cords, and sacrificing small animals just to get the jammed paper unjammed or the wedged paper freed. If all of the usual tactics failed to make the copier work, professionals would have to be called and drastic measures taken.

Seventeen elementary schools, six middle schools, and three high schools would virtually have to shut down without their copiers and the personnel that kept them running. Our district had an entire department who did nothing but service all of the copiers in the district. This department consisted of two men, John and Dave, technical technicians, contraption contractors, mechanism mechanics who were indispensable when good machines went bad.

Together, these two men would show up and act like it was no big deal to turn a few screws and help an ailing copier get up on its rollers again. They seemed unaware of the anxiety that was caused by a machine deciding to take a well-earned but decidedly inconvenient break. Little did they know the apprehension that they eased when they worked their magic on the office copier and it began reproducing again. Once that was done, tempers cooled, blood pressures collectively decreased, and adults became adults again. All participants could breathe easier, have a swallow of caffeine, eat a piece of dark chocolate to calm their nerves, and resume office life.

"May the technological force be with you" is not just a catch phrase; it's an expression of hope and acknowledgement of the metaphysical and ubiquitous power of office technology. Bless you if you work in an office, any office. Bless you for your patience with all the technology that was born to help you but may at times seem more of a hindrance. Remember the days when you didn't have it, the dark days without it. Rejoice in the enlightenment and reassurance of having the miracle copy machine, the incredible computer, and the essential coffeemaker. Where would we be without them?

CHAPTER 3

GUYS WHO GET POCKET PROTECTORS FOR CHRISTMAS

People do no often think of education as a business, but there are many similarities between the two. A business is dictated by money, the bottom line. Schools are also dictated by money. Budgets and budget cuts often affect the way we run things. Businesses try to attract new customers, while schools have a built-in customer base with the children in the neighborhood, but it is also important that they make themselves attractive to parents looking for a better school where they might transfer their student.

A successful business is run by state-of-the-art technology. Schools need the most up-to-date technology to stay on the cutting edge of education. This is how we make sure that even if you can't operate the new television with the universal remote, your junior high student will be able to save the day. As it is in every industry, so is it in education that the people who are the invaluable in the day-to-day operations are the information technology (IT) technicians.

Technology keeps everything running. The hardware (chips) and software (salsa) engineers keep the technology running. My first husband was a software engineer, a rocket scientist for the air force, and although he did not fit in with the pocket-protector crowd, all his coworkers did, and I spent enough time with them to get to know the engineering experts quite well.

One thing that I learned over sixteen years in the main office is that IT guys are strange creatures that sometimes have a difficult time working with the human element of society. They tend to live in a world of their own where you calculate a tip for a meal on your iPhone to exactly 15 percent and leave a ninety-cents tip for a $6.00 lunch. They do not speak of sports or hobbies because neither hold any interest for them, but on a good day, you may get a conversation about the weather.

From just the name alone, information technology, you would assume that these guys would be the best at sharing information and communicating with others, but you would surely be mistaken in that assumption. They actually relate to machines better than human beings. When it comes to computers, they understand everything about the contraptions that can be the curse of any office if they aren't working correctly.

These are the guys who come to the office when your computer is ill, when it freezes up and refuses to do the job it was hired to do. You've tried everything you can think of, and you still get the "program is not responding" message. It's at times like this that I wanted to challenge my computer to a game of sorts. I knew that it could beat me at chess, but I am pretty sure that I would triumph in a kickboxing match, just barely.

Let's face it, the computers going down turned the whole office into a panic room and the following stanza applied: "When in trouble, when in doubt, run in circles scream and shout!" This usually fixed even the most difficulty problem, but when it didn't, the IT technician swooped in to save the day.

The technician was different; he didn't panic. He was as patient with the machine as a parent is with a wayward child. He enters and stands over it with his knuckles on his chin, giving it the perfect you-know-what-you've-done look, and the machine perks up. Then he gives it an it's-unacceptable look, then it makes a miraculous recovery and works perfectly for him!

What? Do these guys go to school to learn this skill, or is it inherent in their DNA?

Each school in the district had their own IT technician. Usually, they were divided up so that there was one guy for every two or three schools. Pretty thinly spread when you think about it because there was always a disobedient computer in one school or another, sometimes all three at once.

Our IT guy was named Cal. I am sure if the district had a technology committee, Cal would have been the chairman. Cal, in a word, was . . . awkward. Not to say he was a nerd, but he always wore short-sleeved, plaid shirts with one pocket, and I am sure that he was a guy that was totally comfortable wearing a pocket protector he had received for Christmas with white tape holding his thick glasses together at the bridge of his nose. Cal had terrible eyesight, and when looking through a door or a window, he would literally press his nose against the glass to peer in, and when holding a sheet of paper in order to read it, he would hold it right against his face.

I was amused and felt bad for him all at the same time. I would often find him waiting outside the office with his forehead resting against the window, looking in to see if we were there. Video would later reveal that Cal had been there since six thirty that morning; school doors didn't open until 8:00 a.m.

Cal was a large lumbering guy. Tall and stout, not chunky, just solid. He was tall enough that he actually ducked when he walked through the door, not because he was going to bump his head, just because it was close and he *thought* he would bump it. He was ungainly with absolutely no sense of urgency whatsoever in any situation. His take was, "I'll take care of things in my own way and in my own time, and things will work out or they won't."

What a technical glitch was to me, it was human error to Cal. He would always tell the kids, "Respect your parents. They graduated without the use of Wikipedia or Google."

Why couldn't we have had Alex, the new, young, hot technician with the dark curly hair as our designated tech? Cal was more like Droopy Dog. If you recall, the MGM animated basset hound cartoon character of the Northwest Hounded Police was an anthropomorphic dog with a droopy face, hence the name Droopy. Both Cal and Droopy possessed the puppy-dog eyes and saggy jowls. Both moved lethargically and could be described as dreary. They both spoke slowly in a nasal-thick monotone voice. Their similarities were remarkable. Like Droopy Dog, Cal was hardly an imposing character, but he was shrewd enough to outwit any computer and fix nearly any software problem, if you had the time to wait on him.

Cal was one of those not-so-well-rounded engineering types that would actually bring up titbits of info like yottabytes in conversation, which I am sure other engineers did. If you don't have any idea what a yottabyte, do not feel alone. I thought it was a small protein bar that Yoda ate for dinner in *Star Wars*. It is actually an astronomical number of bytes or storage for digital information on your computer, literally a quadrillion bytes, and that's a mouthful. I learned this from Cal. His mind was like the proverbial iron trap full of numbers, stats, and equations of all sorts.

With approximately one thousand students and four computer labs, not to mention nearly eighty more computers for teachers and staff, the need for IT support was huge in our school. With the demand that just our school alone had, you might think the district would give us our very own technician. Sadly, this was not the case. The techs that weren't in the schools everyday would be on the other end of the phone at the Help Desk in the district office. So if you called with a problem, you might have reached the tech that serviced your school.

On Cal's first day at the Help Desk, his big size-12 shoe hit a power switch under the desk and shut everything down until someone came to figure out that the surge protector had been switched off. Cal would come to see us once a week, every Wednesday. So we would save up every computer issue in the building, at least the ones that could wait until Droopy, I mean Cal, would show up.

If we had an urgent problem or emergency on a Thursday, the day after we'd last seen Cal, we would have to call his cell and try to contact him to help us over the phone. This was a very frustrating exercise in patience on my part and futility on his.

Cal came lumbering in on a Wednesday in December for a look-see at a computer that had been misbehaving since the preceding Monday, and wouldn't you know it, the computer worked just fine while he was there.

"Just give me a call if it happens again," he uttered.

That same computer refused to even turn on the following Friday. So I e-mailed my faithful IT technician, let him know the dilemma, and asked him to give me a call. He was busy and didn't get back to me right away, but eventually he did call me back. When I told him the difficulty I was having, he listened intently and then responded,

"What do you mean it won't turn on?"

Seriously?

"Well," I began, "when I push the Power button nothing happens."

This was followed by silence. A lengthy, clumsy silence that continued so long I was afraid that we'd been disconnected. Finally, he said,

"Have you checked the plug to make sure it is getting power?"

The trusty plug ploy. He'd had experience with this one.

"Yes, I have done that. I even unplugged it then plugged it back in, good and tight."

"And it still doesn't work?" he asked in his best Droopy Dog voice.

"Right," I said simply.

I was so glad that I was on the phone and not standing face-to-face with him right then because I gave an are-you-kidding-me eye roll that was totally involuntary.

"Okay . . . so . . . nothing," he listlessly stated.

Was this guy for real? I thought to myself, not for the first time. Trying to be patient, again I said, "Right." Then I waited and waited, and as I waited, a miracle happened: my computer flashed, just for a millisecond, and then it flashed again. I gasped and exclaimed,

"A light just flashed!"

Without missing a beat or hesitating at all, he quickly asked, "What color?"

Dumbfounded, I said, "WHAT?"

Unfazed, he repeated, "What color is it flashing?"

Now it was my turn to be silent; actually, it was more like speechless.

"What possible difference can it make what color it is when it flashes?" I screamed inside my head.

Outwardly, in a very calm almost resigned voice, I said to him, "Cal, I didn't catch the color."

"Okay. Okay," he started saying over and over; now he was very animated in a Droopy Dog sort of way. It was clearly his moment to shine.

"I'll be right there." And with that, he hung up, and I was left holding the phone to my ear like an idiot.

"Oh boy, he will be right here," I repeated to no one particular.

As it turned out, Cal was already at a nearby school and was coming through the door in a matter of minutes to examine the naughty machine. He studied and worked and worked and studied the computer. It seemed he was in a chess match with the machine. He spent two and a half hours working and reworking the problem. He had handheld devices, the likes I'd never seen before, plugged into my machine and could not find anything specifically wrong with the hard drive; it just wouldn't turn on and stay on. I have had coworkers with the same problem.

I was beginning to think that my IT guy was as dumb as I was. The day came to a close, and Cal was no closer to solving the dilemma. He would have to come back the next day even though it was not our designated day. He felt the issue was "too important" to wait another week. I guess failure isn't an option; it just comes bundled with the software.

The conclusion to the computer dilemma was that the machine itself was defective and needed to be replaced. I secretly wondered if it was the actual hardware that was faulty or if it could be our geeky IT technician that was faulty and needed to be replaced. Hey, it was a valid question.

CHAPTER 4

NOW, FOR YOUR VIEWING PLEASURE

I dearly loved the majority of my coworkers in the office at school. For the most part, they were funny and genuine, and we had such a wonderful time working together. Of course, we had ups and downs, good bosses and not-so-good bosses, and secretaries that could be difficult and trying, but I learned something valuable from everyone with whom I worked and spent the majority of my waking hours. The first boss I had at my very first school never even knew my name. I was hired by the librarian, whom I still share a great friendship with, and the principal. My boss's boss was just a name on the office door. I only met him a time or two passing in the hallway, but I don't recall hearing a lot of great and inspiring things about him, but since I didn't know him personally, I tried to reserve judgment.

My second boss at the district, a high school principal, was for the most part easy enough to work for, save for one small habit. He would sit at his desk and read about something that another high school was doing or come up with some concept on his own that he would like to instigate in our school. Mostly, these were fun or inspiring things that would make the student population better in some way. Usually, they were just a sketch or a glimpse of an idea that he would then turn over to me to accomplish, but always it meant a project in the making for me and my staff. These were the five words that unsettled me the most in my job: "Hey, I have an idea!" He'd excitedly bellow from behind his desk in the adjacent office.

Not all his ideas would get off the ground, but once in a while, we would find one that would soar for many years because it was so popular with the students.

One of my favorites of these many projects was choosing a book that was given to every graduating senior (three to four hundred) each May. These were usually children's books that the kids probably hadn't read since they really were kids, but they all had a message pertinent to a graduate. A few I can remember were Dr. Seuss's *Oh, the Places You'll Go* and *The Dot* and *Ish* by Peter Reynolds.

Each year, it was a new book, and it was always fun to go to a bookstore and read the many children's books of my past and my children's pasts and look at some new classics to find just the right one that would have the special message he was looking for. The best part of this was that we both were involved in the process because he liked to have hands-on and pick the book that was *the one*. They were important to him, and because he had handpicked them and signed each one with a personal message, they were meaningful to the seniors.

Another of my favorites in regard to these ventures that he began in our school was the Shout-Out Window. This was a four-by-six-foot window near the front office where the students could post shout-outs to teachers for something special.

This particular scheme presented a few problems, like the pencils always being stolen from the table and the necessity to prescreen the notes before they were put up. We didn't want the wrong type of communication going up there. You might believe that some of the comments that went up on the window from these high schoolers would be sarcastic, rude, or insolent. On the contrary, for the most part, with a few exceptions, these shout-outs were fun, complimentary, and positive; both the students and the teachers enjoyed them.

They were written on three-by-three-inch Post-it notes that the kids would scrawl their messages on, then bring them to someone in the office for review. After they were screened, they would be posted

in the window for the world to see. This was always a highlight that I could show parents who were touring our school as a prospective institution for their high-school student to attend. They liked to read what the teachers were doing that the kids loved, and the positive comments were beneficial.

It wasn't long before the teachers were putting up remarks praising other teachers and staff members for jobs well done. Luckily, we did not need to screen these remarks. Some were light and funny; others were serious and heart-felt. The optimism spread through the building, making for a positive environment for both staff and students. Today this would probably be done on a webpage.

About halfway through my tenure for the school district in the main office, said district opted for a change to our school. Not just new trash receptacles or a new coat of drab paint but a building makeover! In fact, a new building altogether. It was to be built on our soccer field, then we would collectively move into the new school and create a new soccer field where the old building was.

Now that I write it on paper, it all seems so easy. I assure you it was not. The move was supposed to take place over the summer vacation. There would be no kids underfoot and no learning taking place. In March, we learned that the contractors were behind on their timetable, which really came as no surprise, so we were now pushed back to a September finish, which meant a move after the school year had already started. The good news was we were getting a brand-new school and everyone was eager and elated.

One person was so excited that they resorted to arson. That's correct; there were two fires set in the building while it was still under construction, so again, we were pushed back on our moving date. Now we were well into November territory, and we could feel the worst coming.

Someone suggested that we wait until January, when all the kids would be around and we could have them carrying boxes and such. However, the district said, "Definitely not." The students could not even be around when the move finally took place. So we were forced to move over winter break. Not only would we be moving over our much-needed break from anything related to school, but we would

be doing it in the cold, snowy, wintery month of December. Merry Christmas, everyone.

Back then we could actually say, "Merry Christmas."

Move we did into our new digs, our pad, our lodge of learning. Our new building was open and airy and delightful with a lot of windows and natural light. It was industrial and retro all at once, not your one-room schoolhouse of old. It was complete with all the technology that was needed in public education today for learning to take place.

Smart Boards were put up in place of traditional blackboards, and Elmos, which were wireless projectors that allowed teachers to control the computer and manipulate images from anywhere in the room, took the place of outdated overhead and overheating projectors. An intricate bell system that could be heard throughout the neighborhood was installed.

It would play music that began thirty seconds before the tardy bell rang, so the kids knew exactly how long they had to reach their classrooms on time, and housewives throughout the neighborhood could set their clocks by it and be apprised as to when to change the laundry and take the cookies out of the oven.

We could actually rotate between the music that we wanted to play during the in-between-class passing-time. Our top favorites were the *Mission Impossible* theme, the *Jeopardy* game show song, and my personal favorite, the *William Tell Overture*, which really got the kids and the stay-at-home moms hurrying. Even I moved faster when I heard it playing.

We also had a complex PA system throughout the building that featured a panic button in every room. Supposedly these were installed so if a teacher needed help right away for any reason, the panic button could be depressed and the calvary would come a-runnin'. The only thing I can say about the panic buttons is that it is a good thing they weren't emergency ejection buttons that could catapult a student out of a breakaway hatch in the roof. Because if they had been, we would have had several students a week literally expelled from the school.

There wasn't a student in the student body that could resist pushing that button. They were supposed to be placed inconspicuously, where only the teachers knew where they were located; nonetheless, the kids would always find them somehow, someway. I will admit that there were a few times when the alarms would be accidental where something or someone would be pushed against them, and sometimes the teachers really did need immediate help, but the majority of the pushes were some student wondering what that little button was for.

Just like the movies, he or she would invariably push it before a conscientious adult could yell, "Don't push that!"

As you know, if you are a parent or a teacher, or both, you can't label this sort of thing. Marking it with a Do Not Push sign would have been too irresistible, and it would have been pushed twice daily instead of the weekly two or three "accidental" presses.

Of course, there were so many good things that came from the move to our new schoolhouse and many things that were much needed. One of these was a new state-of-the-art camera system to monitor the hallways and secluded areas of the building. Oh boy! The first year that we had it, the students were totally unaware of the new surveillance method. We, in the office, were like spies performing espionage on the student body. We weren't even undercover. We were scouting right out in the open, gathering intelligence and evidence needed to make the kids spill their guts on their misbehaving, law-breaking, no-good classmates.

It never ceased to amaze me why they didn't learn we were watching. Okay, the first year I can see how it might be a surprise that the whole office knew you were spitting from the balcony on the second floor or making out in the gymnasium. You would think that after the first semester, word would spread, and everyone would know and try to avoid the cameras. Nope, each year, new kids would come in, and the students from the past years would still be getting into trouble and still be getting caught on camera.

I have to admit I took some delight in a boy coming in to the office and Mr. Montgomery, the assistant principal, asking him what he knew about a certain act and him lying through his teeth, denying

even the possibility that he was somehow involved in such an abhorrent scheme and then finding out that the whole episode was caught on camera like a bad sitcom.

Mr. M would call the unsuspecting rule breaker into his office and shut the door behind him, striking fear into the heart of the boy. He would always give them ample opportunity to come clean. He'd always start by saying,

"I am going to ask you a question, and before you answer, consider that I already know the truth."

This not only frightened the mischief maker, but it always got him thinking, *What could he possibly know, and how could he possibly know it?*

Cameras! The cameras were the answer!

"All of you know we have cameras in every part of the building!" I wanted to shout every time.

They even put cameras in the buses, for heaven's sake, to catch the kids trying to throw one another out of a window or exchanging clothing in the back seat or lighting the floor on fire. The ones in trouble were so busy trying to figure out Mr. M's superpower of knowledge that they usually gave up the rest of the story quicker than Paul Harvey. Before they even knew what was happening, they had sung like a proverbial bird, as they say in the cop dramas.

Boy, we really could have used this technology when we were conducting our candy contest in the library. We had a large jar of jelly beans at the checkout counter, and the only rule was whoever could guess the number of beans in the jar would win the entire lot. That was until one student decided that he or she didn't need to guess the number; all they needed to do was sneak into the library and steal the whole jar, jelly beans and all.

But now, we had cameras and monitors to catch the little fiends! Our halls and our jelly beans would now be safe.

We mounted a television monitor in the main office on the wall in front of my desk. It was in plain sight, but very few parents or students saw it because they would face me when they stood at my desk and the screen was behind them above their heads. We could see virtually every part of the school from that monitor, and in the

afternoons, it was just like turning on a soap opera in the middle of the day that made you want to get comfy and grab some bonbons to watch.

I would fire it up, ready all the cameras, and on cue, the magnificent equipment would whir to life, and the lenses would begin rotating through every hallway, classroom, and isolated corner of the school, just waiting to catch someone doing something they shouldn't be doing.

One afternoon, an English teacher called down to the office to explain that she had a student who was not feeling well and had left her classroom to go to the restroom and then down to the office. She had been gone quite some time, and the teacher wanted to know if she'd made it to the office yet. She was beginning to worry.

"Could you keep an eye out for her?" she asked.

"Of course!" I said, and I flipped on the monitor above my desk. "And now for your viewing pleasure!" I announced in my best game-show-announcer voice.

A few short minutes later, we saw poor little sick Casey coming down the hall. Only she didn't really look sick. In fact, she was singing and dancing and twirling around, making her approach down the hall to the main office seem rather merry. When she reached the top of the stairs just above us, she stopped, composed herself, slumped her shoulders, hung her head, and grabbed the railing on the stairs with both hands for dramatic effect.

We watched, first on the screen and then in person as she came into view on the stairway. She staggered in through the doors and sank into a chair, trying to catch her breath.

"I am having trouble breathing," she gasped.

What a performance! I wanted to stand and applaud, giving her the standing ovation she so richly deserved.

"Bravo!" I wanted to shout. "Sign her up for theater!"

I really wanted to tell her that her breathing problem was probably due to the dancing, but instead, I told her to have a seat and Mr. Montgomery would be with her in a minute.

"I need to call my mom to come and get me," she whimpered.

"I am sure he will help you with that," I said. "You look pretty sick and may need him to talk to her."

I know, I'm a scamp, but I couldn't help it. Mr. M had watched the whole show. He gave me a quick wink as he showed her into his office. I so wanted to be there when he replayed the video of her singing and dancing her way to the main office so I could have witness her reaction. Instead, I would have to wait for Mr. M's recap.

"She hemmed and hawed and stammered, and she just couldn't believe it," he said, unable to believe that she'd been coming to this school for two years and she still didn't know that we had cameras to look out for this sort of thing. *We* couldn't believe *that*.

However, nothing could beat the comedy of errors that was the group of boys that had a permanent marker and were taking turns drawing on the brand-new blond brick of our building. Their creation started small, then as they each had a turn, they got braver, and the picture went from silly to dirty and got bigger and bigger in a manner of speaking.

We did not have the chance to watch these Rembrandts at work, or we could have stopped them before they finished. It was only after we discovered their artistic prowess on the wall that we could go back to the cameras and catch them in the act—so to speak, really it was after the act. These little darlings sat at Mr. M's desk and denied that they even knew what a permanent marker was or what one looked like.

He tried his old trick. "I already know the answer," he said, "so you might as well tell me."

But they were steadfast in their denials. It wasn't until they saw the video of themselves drawing like it was their job, giggling like schoolgirls, and photographing the completed work so they could later post it on social media that they realized the depth of trouble they were in. The writing was on the wall, one might say.

The best part was that we had the video to show their parents when the inevitable words "My boy would never do that. He knows we would ground him for life" were spoken.

The video was reviewed, then they had no choice but to confess. Their punishment was to scrub the brick until the obscenities

were gone. Have you ever tried removing permanent maker from brick? They were going to be scrubbing for a long, long time.

Yes, the cameras were wonderful things that captured our hearts and a few thieves as well. They weren't just entertainment. They were *advantageous* entertainment. Expedient and worth every penny it cost to install them. They were helpful in keeping order, and we hoped the kids would someday figure out we had them and try to stay out of trouble. Yeah, right.

PART TWO

PEOPLE WHO NEED
PEOPLE ARE THE
LUCKIEST PEOPLE

CHAPTER 5

MR. SMITH GOES TO MIDDLE SCHOOL

It is a bright Monday morning in the second month of school. The time is 8:22 a.m. Classes started two minutes earlier. A man walks quickly down the long hallway toward the administrative offices of the Middle School. He is a plain man about forty years old with an uncharacteristic face, thinning mouse-brown hair, and small wire-rimmed glasses. He walks determinedly with his head down and his torso tilted forward, giving the impression that his legs and feet are trying to catch up with his upper body. He holds the hand of a very small boy in the seventh grade who looks as though he should still be attending elementary school. He is a man that the staff in the main office will come to know well but not necessarily come to love, only barely to tolerate. His name is Mr. Smith.

His son, the boy he leads by the hand, is Samuel Michael Smith, who has just been admitted to our school's special education (SPED) program, which accepts children from all over the valley. He will not be in a self-contained special education class, but rather, he will attend a low-to-moderate disability mainstreamed class with a modified curriculum and remedial instruction. This was in line with our district policies and the Individuals with Disabilities Education Act (IDEA).

As Mr. Smith enters the office, I greet him warmly and welcome him and Sam to the boy's new school. He looks at me, blinks a cou-

ple of times as he informs me matter-of-factly that the clock in our office is two minutes early, and asks if we could fix them to reflect the correct time. It was now my turn to blink a few times and stand speechless only because I didn't know what to say to his response to my greeting.

Finally, I manage to speak, "Sure. I will pass it along to our custodial staff."

This seems to appease him for the moment, and he launches into an explanation of why he is here even though I already know. We have been expecting Sam and are happy to have him.

From that day forward, Mr. Smith was always in the building. He learned the procedures of the office very quickly. Visitors must sign in at the front desk before going anywhere else in the building. He took this rule extremely seriously. Even if he was only dropping Sam off or picking him up, whether he was in the school for ten seconds or ten minutes, Mr. Smith would come in and go directly to the visitor's log to fill in the information required and have us make a stick-on "visitor's tag" for him to wear on the front of his shirt.

Then he would roam the halls, stroll through the cafeteria, interrupt classes, and generally make a nuisance of himself. Mr. Smith also got into the routine of coming to the building during the school day to hang out in front of whatever classroom Sam was in. He would sneak in the SPED wing's special entrance, then loiter outside the classrooms where Sam could see him and disrupt the entire wing. The teachers complained and made requests to have him banned to the office. If they only knew how much time he was already spending in the office, they would have never suggested such a thing. Every day we would go through this ritual; this habit alone could drive the main office personnel to drink more than just Diet Coke. He was asked to leave the building during the school day.

I wanted to put my arm around Mr. Smith's shoulders and tell him,

"Just go home, Stan. We will take care of Samuel Michael Smith, and all will be well until the end of school."

After many requests by the SPED teachers begging her to rectify the problem, Mrs. Graham, our principal, told him that he could

not wander the special education wing and it would be appreciated if he would remain outside rather than linger in the building. To make this point, that entrance was locked to outside visitors as soon as the first tardy bell of the day sounded. All doors, except the front door to the school, remained locked throughout the day. We could watch the main entrance, so if Mr. Smith tried to gain entry (or I should say *when*), Mr. Montgomery, the assistant principal, could have a word with him.

Mr. Smith learned to call the office because he knew that we could open any door from that location and he'd request that we open the door and let him in. If we didn't open the door, he would prowl the physical boundary of the school, systematically testing it for weaknesses. Just like the velociraptors in *Jurassic Park* tested the fences for an escape, Mr. Smith was trying to get into the school any way he could. He found that weak link at a door in the back of the gym left open for deliveries. He began using that door to sneak into the school and tiptoe toward Sam's classroom. Again, he was asked to leave the building; the man was impossible. Once he was exiled to the out of doors, he soon began to follow Sam around to his classes and look in through the windows in each of the boy's classrooms.

For crying out loud!

He was relentless about the clocks in the main office and the two-minute time change. Apparently, it was throwing his entire life schedule off. He would call to find out if the clocks had been changed. Even after they were changed, he would call to check the time they were showing to make sure it was in sync with his watch. The phone would ring, and upon answering it, the first question I would hear would be, "What time do you have?" Then he would repeat it to you while writing it down.

If Mr. Smith wasn't in the office, he would be calling the office. He would sit in front of the school in his car and call us, and he would always start by asking the time, then he would ask the name of the person answering the phone. He would then take the name down in a little notebook, and he would spell everything out loud as he wrote. After the time and the name verification and spelling, he would always say,

"Hello, this is Mr. Smith, Samuel Michael Smith's father. Do you remember me?"

Oh yes, Mr. Smith, we certainly do. He always used Sam's full name so there would be no confusing him with anyone else. Then he would launch into whatever he was calling about, usually some trivial matter that would almost certainly require a great deal of my time. Every day I wanted to ask him, "Don't you have a job? Someplace you need to be or something you should be doing other than bothering us here?"

I never did because I was afraid he would actually answer.

He adopted the habit of arriving at school forty-five minutes early in the morning to make sure he was there when the bell rang. Each morning, he would come early and park outside the special education classrooms where the SPED buses were supposed to drop off their charges. He would then leave his car there so the buses had nowhere to park, and he'd walk the perimeter of the building with Sam in tow. Sun, rain, sleet, or snow, just like a mailman, Mr. Smith and Sam would circle the building until the doors were unlocked and students were allowed to enter. Maybe we should get Mr. Smith an application to work at the post office.

One Thursday morning during breakfast in the cafeteria and before classes had started, I heard my office clerk say, "Uh-oh."

When I looked up from my task, I saw Mr. Smith coming down the hallway, heading straight for the office. He came through the glass doors and went directly to the visitor's sign-in log, but instead of signing in, he looked at me and stated,

"I have something for you."

He seemed almost giddy, which was uncommon for Mr. Smith because he was a pretty serious guy. He had a little mischievous grin on his face, and he kept me in suspense as he proceeded to sign in and watch me fill in his daily visitor's tag. It occurred to me that I really should have had a permanent name tag made just for him. That would have made him feel so important.

Once all this was completed, he reached into his *Despicable Me* backpack, which he always carried, pulled out a sheet of paper, and proudly handed it to me. I looked it over as he explained,

"It's an application to be your head custodian."

"Oh, Lord, no!" I exclaimed aloud.

I couldn't help myself. The involuntary outcry just burst from my lips. It was a pure and honest reaction, but I caught myself and tried to recover.

"I don't think we are hiring right now," I managed weakly.

"The district office informed me that every school is always on the lookout for good custodians," he said.

At that moment, I wanted to put a witch's hex on whoever gave him that impression. Maybe I could send him back to the district office to bother him or her for the remainder of the afternoon or school year. I seriously considered telling him that he had to have the district's superintendent personally sign his application and not to come back without that signature, but I realized that would only put my job in jeopardy, so I reached out to take the application. It was like reaching for a paper that I knew was poisoned and detrimental to my health, because having Mr. Smith working here would be decidedly bad for my health and maybe to his as well.

I took the application from his hand with my fingers shaking and said,

"I will turn this in for you and see that it gets to the person in charge of hiring our custodians."

He seemed happy with my statement, and I did what I'd pledged to do. I turned his application over to our current head custodian and warned him that Mr. Smith was out for his job. He immediately entered it into the circular file by the side of his desk.

After Mr. Smith had applied for a custodian's job at the school (and hadn't gotten one), he seemed set on finding and pointing out all the areas where our current custodial staff were lacking. He was determined to find deficiencies and make us aware of them. To our staff's credit, there were very few glaring examples, but Mr. Smith kept a sharp eye out for each and every one of them. From finding glitter outside the art room on the floor to fingerprints on the doors, he was obsessed in his mission. Just like the clocks in the office, he was relentless in his pursuit of deeming our custodial department incapable so that he could be granted a position therein.

The school year went on and on like this with Mr. Smith trying different excuses for being at school and different approaches for entering the forbidden zone.

He dropped Sam off on a fairly slow Tuesday morning and came into the office to report that there was dust under the stairway leading upstairs.

"You can see the dust bunnies as you walk up the stairs," he informed me.

"Really?" I sarcastically replied. "I think that Tuesday afternoons are the time designated to take care of all dust bunnies in the school."

He was not amused by my humor, nor was he dissuade in his pursuit of dust bunnies. He was nothing if not persistent.

Mr. Smith reminded me of Jimmy Stuart in Lewis R. Foster's *Mr. Smith Goes to Washington*. He was fidgety and bumbling with a quiet voice and a determined mind-set. Instead of fighting the corruption of the political machine in Washington like Jim, our Mr. Smith was fighting against the educational system through the main office of our middle school.

He learned quickly to manipulate that system. For instance, he knew that although it was frowned upon, there was no rule against taking your child out of school before the final bell of the day rang. So Mr. Smith, being the ambitious fellow that he was, would make it his custom to come to the office a few minutes early every day to collect Samuel Michael Smith. He would sign the visitor's log, obtain his visitor's badge, and sit in the office to wait until the busy SPED staff could bring Sam down to go home. For several weeks, he would come to school a minute or two earlier each day until the day came when he would be there forty minutes early, sitting in the office with the name tag on his shirt, waiting for Sam. Finally, Mrs. Graham had to tell him that he could only come five minutes early to take Sam home from then on.

All our special education teachers were required to carry a radio during the day. You never know when something would happen. An autistic child might throw a tantrum or cause an injury, or a child might have a seizure and need immediate attention. Any number of emergencies could occur where the teacher may need assistance, and

the radio was the best way to ensure a quick response. The radio was also handy in other situations as well.

One day, the radio on my desk that was the lifeline to the entire school crackled to life. I was quick to answer in case it was the SPED department needing help.

"Main office, what can I do for you?" I spoke into the microphone part of the walkie-talkie.

"Mr. Smith is in the building!" the panicked voice came back through.

"How did he get in?" one of the other teachers who had a radio on that channel asked.

"I don't know, but he is in the north hallway, heading to the main office."

Suddenly, the registrar had important and immediate work to do in the file room, all the office aides had to use the restroom at the same time, the office clerk had mail that needed to be hand-delivered to the teachers right now, and the counselor picked up her phone to return non-existent calls. I was standing alone with the radio still in my hand and a deer-in-the-headlights look on my face when Mr. Smith entered the office doors. After the signing in process was done and he had his tag on his chest, he said,

"I ran over the chain that you use to block your parking lot at night, and it gave my car a flat tire."

Oh, is that all.

I noted mentally that when I went past the entrance to the parking lot this morning, the chain was lying on the grass on the other side of the post.

"How could you run over the chain?" I asked, afraid of the answer.

"When I got here this morning, there was a big yellow bus parked in my spot, so I went up on the curb, around the post, and over the grass to get to the parking lot. That's when I ran over the chain," he said straight-faced and to the point.

In my mind, I ticked off these points on my fingers: (1) that big yellow bus is the special needs bus, which is supposed to be there, (2) that is not *your* parking place, and (3) YOU'RE NOT SUPPOSED TO

DRIVE ON THE GRASS! I was having serious fantasies about killing Mr. Smith to put us out of our misery. How could I do it and still keep my job? I wondered. How could I put an end to this little mousy man and his neurotic behavior?

Resigned to the fact that Mr. Smith would live and would probably be the end of me, my sanity, and the mental health of the staff, I picked up the phone, dialed the custodian's office, and asked if someone there could help him change his tire. Then I looked at Mr. Smith's little mouse-like face and said,

"The custodians are busy sweeping glitter off the art room floor right now, but when they are done, one of them might be able to help you." I wanted to add, "After they clean up all the dust bunnies," but I didn't.

The end finally did come for Mr. Smith. One cloudy, rainy afternoon, he arrived very early to pick up Sam. It was only 2:15 p.m., earlier than he had ever come before. I eyed him suspiciously. We summoned Sam to the office with his coat and backpack, and Mr. Smith asked,

"If it's not too much trouble, could I please use your restroom?"

"Of course," I answered, leery of his contrite attitude today, and off to the lavatory he went.

A few minutes later, Sam made it down to the office, but there was no sign of his dad yet. So we all waited, Sam with his coat on and the rest of us wondering, *What in the blazes was taking him so long?* The class period ended, and the last class of the day began with Sam waiting and swinging his legs in front of the chair he was sitting in, and still his dad remained indisposed.

As it got closer to three o'clock and the end of the day, we were really getting worried. Something must be wrong in there. A couple of us knocked on the door, but no response came from inside. We were just about to call the EMTs to rescue Mr. Smith from the bathroom when Dick, the head custodian, wandered in with his keys. He knocked, again no response, so he unlocked the door, and the door swung into the small room. There, sitting on the floor was Mr. Smith with the toilet completely taken apart.

There were toilet parts everywhere—handles, valves, screws, unknown parts, and parts I didn't want to know about scattered the floor. He was sitting in the midst of them, I'm sure wondering how in the world he was going to put the damn thing back together. He looked up at us with a look not quite like the cat that swallowed the canary, rather the cat not knowing what to do now that he'd swallowed the canary. He said, with all the confidence he could muster, "Your toilet was broken, so I thought I'd fix it for you."

He looked up tired and defeated and couldn't quite pull off the confidence he was looking for. Dick helped him up off the floor, knowing that he was now going to have to reassemble the toilet. A few calls were made to the district special education director, and the next day, Samuel Michael Smith was withdrawn from our school.

I felt sorry for Mr. Smith. He was just trying to be the best parent he could to Sam even though he made me want to smack my head against my desk sometimes. To say that Mr. Smith was obsessive-compulsive was like saying the *Titanic* had sprung a small leak. He was almost as neurotic as my pet Chihuahua, Jeter. The only difference between them was Jeter would spin around in circles, then lift his leg, and pee on the floor. Mr. Smith hadn't done that, but I was afraid that it could happen in the next school his son attended.

CHAPTER 6

CREATIVE ALPHABETIZING

A middle school English teacher once asked one of her students to say a sentence beginning with *I*. The girl began "I is . . ."

"Stop," implored the teacher, "It's *I am.*"

The girl stopped, looking a bit confused. She continued, "Okay, *I* am the ninth letter in the alphabet."

All the teacher could do was admit her mistake and laugh a bit at herself.

Many times, I have heard the phrase, "I don't even want to think about what they are not teaching you in school."

Tom Hanks said it as Sam, the lonely single dad in the 1993 movie *Sleepless in Seattle*. I have maybe even said it myself a few times. Being a principal's secretary in a middle school, I didn't have classrooms full of students every day, but I did have a dozen students each day as aides to the personnel in the office. This small group of students taught me a lot of good things about the character and quirks of the junior high and high-school-age student. A few of the things they taught me were all the things that they weren't being taught in school.

I don't know when alphabetizing became a lost art. It has probably gone the way of the lost arts of compassion, listening, keeping a secret and conversation, all of which can be attributed to social media. Thanks to the all-powerful cell phone, laptop and tablet, everyone under the age of twenty has lost the ability to converse

face-to-face with another human being. In fact, the number of young adults dating has decreased since the popularization of social media. There is no need to face-to-face converse when we only need to tap a few buttons. Note: Also declining: teenage pregnancies. Hmmm, interesting.

I had to take a public speaking class in college, and I am so thankful every time I have to speak in front of a group of any kind, be it school, church, work, or club affiliations. Most teenagers or young adults would be paralyzed with fear if they had to speak in public. I'm not talking about the intense anxiety caused by lalophobia, the fear of speaking; it's more about being too lazy to be personal.

It's just so much easier to talk to someone via predictive text, and you can write things that you would never say to someone if you are face-to-face. This is why I believe social media to be a pitfall in our society. While it's great to keep in touch with Aunt Agnes across the country, it takes away from a personal call, a visit just across town, or even letter writing. If you're not on Facebook, you are incommunicado. Today's teenagers are learning how *not* to communicate.

When I was a young student, as early as elementary school, my classmates and I would agonize over the three *R*s. Kids today don't even know what the three *R*s represent. We also had to learn cursive writing. They don't even teach cursive in school anymore. I have had students from seventh grade to twelfth grade who cannot read anything written in cursive. They can't write their name unless it is print, and they have no signature. They simply do not know how to sign their names. My eighteen-year-old son will tell me, "I can't read your writing," not because it is particularly messy or fragmented but because it is in cursive.

Spelling and grammar are not totally things of the past; however, these are difficult to teach when you are competing with emojis and SMS and textese. Do U C wht I mean? :{ Twenty-first century teenagers don't know what it means to laugh emphatically unless you write "LMAO" on their screen.

Another fundamental skill that is severely lacking in today's educational process is the lost art of alphabetizing. Learning the alphabet is about one of the first things you learn growing up and

the basic foundation of all you would learn from that time forward. You had memorized your ABCs by three years old, you could sing the catchy alphabet song for all of your parents' friends, and you had reading by the tail. Alphabetizing was a simple skill once known by everyone in the land; all you had to do was recall the alphabet song. Right? Well, maybe not.

I learned one Wednesday morning from my office aides that alphabetizing was not the simple act I thought it was; to be sure, it was a lot more complicated than I thought it ever could be. I am quite sure that these particular students probably went on to decipherer codes for the government or some such similar occupation, but at this point in their young lives, they were about to practice creative alphabetizing.

After registration, we usually had a truckload, literally, of paperwork and forms that would need to be filed. To start on this monumental project, we would begin by having our office aides separate the forms and then alphabetize each group.

Our first group of aids from first and second periods had no problem separating the forms. Success! We were on the right track; we might even be finished by the end of the day. The next group coming in for third period were to begin alphabetizing each set of forms. Victory was not so quick in coming this time.

The third-period aides were two boys and one girl. A couple of them had a handful of letters after their names, letters like ADD and ADHD. We tried to keep them busy and saved tasks to keep them occupied so there was very little downtime for them. The alpha-mission seemed the perfect job to fill their morning before they went to lunch.

They seemed competent and were quite eager to begin, although they were a little unsure of themselves. So before we set them on their task, we took a few minutes to review with them exactly what we wanted. All we had to say was "alphabetize," and their eyes glazed over, their heads cocked slightly to one side, and a look of pure confusion came across all three faces. We originally set out to have them alphabetize about three thousand forms that were in six groups, so about five hundred forms per file. Let me stress that they were *not*

required to do the math. The idea was, we would start by giving them each one pile to alphabetize. In hindsight, this might have been too much for them on their first try.

We moved them into the office conference room, a large room that had all the amenities conference rooms would need to be functional: a large table, eight chairs, and a whiteboard that covered one wall. It had windows as the other three walls so we could observe the work in progress. Thinking they had all they would need to complete the assignment, we returned to our desks and continued working.

Several minutes later, I glanced up from my keyboard and looked through the windows to see what headway had been made. I observed nothing. Zero. No work at all was being done. Not even one piece of paper had been moved from the piles. They were not even shuffling papers, pretending to do the job. They just sat looking back and forth from one to the other with wide-eyed quizzical looks. I walked into the room to find out, "What the heck?" and "What are you guys?"

Upon investigating, it turns out that they were totally unfamiliar with the alphabet. It seemed their main question was, "Which letter should they start with?"

Now it was my turn to cock my head and have a look of complete mystification. Unbelieving the situation was as desperate as it seemed, I wanted to turn this into a learning moment. I went to the whiteboard on the wall and in big red letters, I wrote the alphabet for them *A* to *Z*. Then I underlined the first letter and said,

"You should probably start with the letter *A*."

"*A* am the first letter of the alphabet." See how I used that in a sentence? Proud that I had not lost my composure and thinking that I had accomplished my task and hoping that they would now accomplish theirs, I departed the room and left them to their own devices.

The bell for lunch rang, and they flew out of the conference room like it was a medieval torture chamber they had been kept in for sixty minutes and had miraculously escaped. The office secretaries ventured into the room to find that some of the papers had indeed been alphabetized but only about thirty of the thousands that had to be done. Note to self: alphabetizing was not the forte of the third-pe-

riod aids. Maybe there would be more success with fourth period. I could always hope.

Fourth period came after lunch. The aids were a group of cute, giggly girls who, I was sure, would be very competent alphabetizers. No such luck!

I put them in the conference room to complete the task, but I changed it up just a little bit and told them to just put the piles of papers in groups of *A, B, C,* and so on. Then after that was done, we would alphabetize within each group. It went a little quicker with the girls talking and working and making what seemed to be tons of headway in their task. They had finished nearly two-third of the stack of forms alphabetized into letter groups. There was still some work to be done, but forty-five minutes into the sixty-minute period, we were definitely making progress! When I checked on the girls, I came into the room and began going through the pile created for the letter A.

I quickly realized that something was definitely wrong. None of the forms in the group were names that began with the letter A. There were no Andersons, Adams, Allens, or Andrews. In fact, I couldn't make heads nor tails of any of the work they had done. I asked the other secretary to come in to see what she could make of the quandary. The more we studied, the more confused we became. What the fudge brownies was going on?

When we asked the girls how they had gone about doing the work we had asked of them, they proudly replied,

"We alphabetized each form by the second letter in the first name."

"What?" I gasped

As I looked through the stack I saw they weren't lying, each first name did, in fact, have an A as the second letter. Trying to remain calm, I took a deep breath trying to find my happy place. "Rainbows and puppies," I told myself. I asked, "How did you come up with *that* system?"

"That's just how it's done," was the incredible answer from one of the girls. "Isn't it?" she added after seeing the look of disbelief on my face.

As inconceivable as it might seem that instead of alphabetizing by the first letter of the last name or even the first letter of the first name, these cute, young girls honestly believed that the accepted protocol for alphabetizing was to use the second letter of the individual's first name. Clearly the age at which you lose the skill for alphabetizing, if you even had the alphabetizing gene to begin with, is thirteen. So much for hiring a teenager while they still know everything.

"Well," I began sarcastically, "here we alphabetized by the first letter of the last name."

Needless to say, we explained to the girls the correct way to alphabetize. They gave a valiant effort at arguing their point but in the end realized the wisdom in what we were telling them and left knowing how to put so many papers into alphabetical order. Ours was such a rewarding job!

After they left, we grudgingly looked at all the papers that had been sort of alphabetized and realized how many still needed to be alphabetized for real. We gathered them all into one pile and wondered if we shouldn't just stay late after work and do the task ourselves.

Fifth period arrived with a flurry of new aides eager to help us in some way. Not knowing if we could stand any more help, we put the alphabetizing away because we'd had enough surprises for one day. We gave the fifth period aides the task of sorting the mail and putting it into the faculty mailboxes. We realized too late that the boxes were arranged, you guessed it, alphabetically by the teachers' last names.

It was my job to get them started. This could quickly go downhill. I carefully explained how the boxes were positioned and exactly how to find which box belonged to which teacher. I went so far as to tell them how to tell the difference between the first name and the last name. Bravely, I sent them to the mailroom with a basket full of periodicals, catalogs, letters, and flyers.

I gave them specific instructions: If you can't find the proper box, bring it back to me, and I will come back to help you. Twenty minutes later, the aides returned with the basket still three-quarter full. Patiently but dejectedly, I walked back to the mailroom to help.

I began the training anew. "The name on this letter is Adam Hall, so this one goes into the box marked Mr. Hall."

"What if the box doesn't have a name on it?" Henry asked sincerely.

Trying hard to keep a straight face and still remaining patient, I replied,

"If the box doesn't have a name on it, then no mail will be put in there. Okay, now you try it."

Henry picked up a magazine from the basket, looked and the label, and promptly tossed it into the box with no name. Grrrr! I made eye contact with him and spoke very slowly.

"Why would you put that mail into that box with no name?"

"Well, there wasn't a name on the box, and I wasn't sure who the person on the label is, so . . ." His little voice trailed off, and he finished with a shrug.

I stared at him incredulously lost in that adult place, halfway between laughing and crying, halfway between hugging and violence; fighting the urge to give in to my frustration. I removed the magazine from the box and explained once more that if no name is on the box, no mail goes into it.

"Whose name is on the magazine label?" I asked.

He looked at me and said, "Yours."

"So where does it go?" I coaxed.

I looked at the box that was labeled with my name. The question was hopeful and full of anticipation, expectation, and faith. Henry, that sweet, quiet boy looked me directly in the eye and said,

"Here you go."

He handed the magazine to me and walked away. His work here was done.

CHAPTER 7

THERE'S NO SUBSTITUTE FOR A GOOD SUBSTITUTE

Everyone remembers the DeLorean from the 1985 classic movie *Back to the Future*. The cool-looking auto that reached 88 mph and did magical things. What you may not know about that car is, although it looked cool, it is on every list out there for being one of the worst-running cars to come out of the eighties. It's not really helpful that it looks great if it doesn't run smoothly.

Whenever I would tell people I was a principal's secretary at a public school, generally their response would be this: "Oh, you must run the school then."

I would always reply, "No, I just try to make it run smoothly."

Because it doesn't matter if it looks efficient, the school has to run efficiently to make it flow, no matter what else happens, or the school year will not be a success. While the principals and assistant principals do the heavy lifting, budgeting, hiring, curriculum, and discipline, it's their secretaries that keep the pistons going up and down and the engine running smoothly, so to speak and without a hitch.

A good school secretary knows *everything* that is happening in her building, from which teacher is having a bad day and why to how many textbooks the math department is going to need next year. She conquers scheduling, supplies, first aid, complaints, planning, operations, ways, means, and appropriations, all while fixing boo-boos,

leaping tall buildings, and landing on her high heels. She can sign for a package, hold an anxious teacher's hand, wipe a runny nose, and catch a dodgeball all at the same time. I'm not saying she's a super-hero, but why isn't someone making a blockbuster Hollywood movie about these gals and their mad skills?

Just think what she could accomplish if she were like Leonardo da Vinci, who was known as a Renaissance man because he was a painter, architect, inventor, and could write with both hands at the same time. There are accounts of the time that reveal that Leonardo could draw with his left hand while wring a mirrored script at the same time with his right. Holy ambidextrous, Batman! He would have made a great school secretary. I mean just the painting on his back thing alone would qualify him, or was that Michelangelo?

One of the hardest things I did when I was a secretary in the main office was step in when five teachers called in sick and only three of the open slots were filled by district substitutes. All you need to do is step into a classroom with thirty-five teenagers to gain a new respect for not only the teaching profession but the thousands of substitutes who daringly face that fracas every day.

As in every profession, there are great teachers, and there are teachers who probably should be Willie Burgers managers. When you are a teacher, there are certain things that you should do, and then there are things that you should steer clear of.

Having the kids in your chemistry class try making their own root beer without the premade mix from the store is one thing you should do. It's a fun learning experience even if the root beer at the end is usually undrinkable because it tastes like warm carbonated yeast. It's a positive thing, and what teenager doesn't relate to soda pop?

Presenting a Bible to the teacher across the hall from you then telling her, "God and I are keeping an eye on you." Might be something that you probably shouldn't do.

Encouraging your welding shop students to make fun yard decorations and enter them in the state fair is something that you should do. It enhances their skills and builds their self-esteem—the essence of what teaching is all about.

Commiserating with a student about how tough school is and calling the principal a "miserable ****" might be one of those things you shouldn't do. You may find yourself sitting across from his desk at a later date as he reads those words back to you from a letter that student wrote to him.

If you are a secretary with some extra time on your hands, you should do something positive and productive for the school, like creating a Hall of Fame for any famous people that graduated from your school—such as people doing great things in the community or going on to be sports figures or celebrities.

If you are a secretary holding a grudge against a coworker, you probably shouldn't keep tabs on when they come and go, how long they take for lunch, when they leave after work, or where they park. Now you're just a stalker.

When the teachers can't be in their classrooms or at their schools, for whatever reason, it is nice to have the luxury of substitute teachers. Just like teachers, they can be fantastic or the definition of awful. The substitute teacher has always been and forever will be the brunt of many jokes and the victim of many gags in the classroom. Although I have not personally witnessed it, I have heard horror stories about students pretending to have seizures in class or pretending to be asleep, snoring obnoxiously. Students are always trying to "get one over" on the substitute, and these brave men and women are willing to subject themselves to this for the sake of education.

Hey, he or she is new to the school and new to the rules, so the kids figure, why not? What they don't realize is that most schools run pretty much the same and have basically the same rules, and these guys and dolls have been substitutes before. They know where they are, what they are in for and what they are doing. So, students, beware.

Of all the jokes out there are about substitute teachers, this is the one I enjoy the most:

A substitute teacher at a middle school is in the hallway leaning against a bank of lockers with his head resting on a locker door murmuring, "How did you get yourself into this?"

A secretary happens along and asks, "Are you all right?"

To which the young substitute answers, "I'm not sure. I will let you know as soon as I get this boy out of his locker."

In theory, the substitute teacher should follow any guidelines given by the absentee teacher, provide instruction, encourage the progress of the students, and manage learning in the classroom. In practice, the substitute tries to follow guidelines set by the absentee teacher, tries maintain order, tries to give the students meaningful direction, and tries to make it to lunch without a major, career-ending incident or injury.

At the same time, teachers have dos and don'ts. Substitutes have their own sizable lists of dos and don'ts. Surprisingly enough, neither wearing a bulletproof vest nor taking valium before class is on the "do" list; however, showing up, preferably on time, not cussing, and wearing deodorant are at the top of that list.

When I first started at the school district, back when Jesus was a baby, the only qualification you needed to be a substitute teacher was a high school diploma, and you had to pass a background check. Pretty broad strokes. We had substitute teachers coming in that had just graduated with our senior class the year before. Needless to say, more socializing was going on and less teaching and learning. It was also pretty uncomfortable in the faculty lounge with last year's students joining in on the conversations that sometimes happen in faculty lounges. It was a little weird, to say the least.

In the last century, though, changes have been made in the quest for suitable substitutes for your children. In our state, you now have to have a bachelor's degree of some kind to join the ranks of substitute teachers. But, you might muse, if I have a bachelor's degree of some kind, I probably have better prospects than being a substitute teacher. True story, but if you are out of work, between jobs, looking to make a career change, or just killing time, it's really not a bad gig. I have heard in other states you need to pass a test, like the post office test, before you can be a substitute teacher. I have never seen or taken it, but I would guess this is like a "common sense" type of test. In this case, we might truly be in a world of serious trouble.

The dos and don'ts of substitute teaching are mostly common-sense things, the stuff most people just know. You might think when a sub shows up to work at the school and there is no roll, they might just take the names down on a piece of paper and turn that in to the main office until the official roll is delivered. It's obvious, right?

However, you might be surprised at the uncommon senseless things that some substitutes will do in this exact situation. They will call the main office every five minutes, requesting the roll be delivered because they don't know what to do without it, or they might send groups of students down to the office to find out where the ding-dang roll is. Substitutes do the darndest things in the name of teaching kids.

One of the first dos of substitute teaching: teach only what is on the curriculum.

A sub-T (substitute teacher) has a specific job. Usually, they are given criteria to follow, if not exact instructions. We had a sub-T come in early in November to cover a history / social studies class, and it wasn't long into the day when we had students and teachers near that classroom coming to the office to report "bizarre behavior" happening therein.

When the vice principal went to investigate the classroom antics, he found the sub-T standing on the desk, giving a stump speech to the eighth graders about politics, lecturing on the flaws of our government, and giving her opinion on who they should vote for in the upcoming election. I guess she didn't realize that these kids were only twelve years old, and it would be another six years and at least one more president before they could cast their ballots. They thought a conservative was someone who turned off the lights and didn't let the water run while brushing his or her teeth. Nevertheless, she was giving it her all, and they were mesmerized watching her rhetoric and speech-making from high atop her desk.

Of course, the administrator asked her to cease with the flamboyant oration and put a stop to her show.

"Please stick to the history curriculum," he advised. "I'm sure the teacher left notes for you to follow."

"These kids are never going to learn anything from another presidential word-search puzzle," she protested. "They need someone who knows the downfalls of their government to inform them."

She was definitely pushing her political agenda on the young, unsuspecting audience who sat staring at her with wide eyes and dropped jaws as she threw out tired political clichés and hyperbole from her soapbox or desktop, as it were. At the end of the day, all the students were talking about her, and the faculty and staff were debating her viewpoints as well. If nothing else, she got the school buzzing about the impending election. In the office, we were putting in a request that she not be sent back to our school again.

Another "do" in substitute teaching: stay awake in class.

Our principal, Mrs. Graham, made it a habit of visiting four or five classrooms each day to keep in touch with both the students and the teachers. As our drama teacher, Mr. Horace, was out sick, she decided to visit his classroom. When she entered his room, the kids were out of control and bouncing off the walls, literally. She scanned the classroom for the teacher and soon located him sound asleep at the teacher's desk. Now, I don't know how long it's been since you were in a classroom full of thirty 12-year-old drama students, but let me remind you—the disorder and noise level rivals the pandemonium of a rock concert. The fact that this man could even sleep through the noise was amazing.

Mrs. G pushed her way to the front of the class, and as soon as some of the students noticed her, the noise died down almost immediately. A hush fell over the room, and they knew they were in for it, but more importantly they knew that *he* was in for it. She made her way to the desk and found the simple quiz that the kids were supposed to be taking. After a quick but stern lecture about classroom behavior, she got them started. The snoozing sub still didn't wake up. She tried to rouse the deep-sleeper by first tapping him on the shoulder and then by shaking him, almost violently. Finally, he opened his sleepy eyes and looked confused about where he was exactly.

"Welcome back, Mr. Substitute," she said sarcastically. "We hope we didn't disturb your slumber."

He blinked a couple of times and then realized, just as the students had a few minutes earlier, he was in some hot water.

"Oh, s-sorry," he stammered. "I was up so late working my other job that I just needed a little nap." He said it like it was a totally acceptable and appropriate excuse for sleeping in class.

I think she should have made him sit in the principal's office for the rest of the day, but instead, Mrs. G sent him home without his pay for the day, and she covered the class for the remaining periods. Imagine having the principal teaching your history class; the kids loved it! They were fond of her and felt comfortable having her in their classroom. The substitute, however, was not invited back.

The key to a useful substitute, aside from quick thinking on your feet, is to be prepared. Our financial literacy teacher was about to go on a cruise for her twentieth wedding anniversary, and two weeks in advance, she had requested a specific substitute for her class while she was away. This woman had been a substitute for us before, and we looked forward to her coming to our building again. It was near the end of the calendar year, and winter break was just around the corner. Many teachers and substitutes alike were gearing down—meaning, the closer to the holidays we got, the less actual work the students were required to do.

So in the holiday spirit of things, the sub-T for the financial literacy class decided to show a movie to the kids. A movie, she thought, that would teach them something about finances, like the stock market, and which might also contain some holiday cheer. Her choice: *Trading Places*, with Dan Aykroyd and Eddie Murphy. Okay, before you go off thinking, *What the Ebenezer Scrooge was she thinking?* it *was* a movie about commodity trading and social hierarchy, and the plot *did* unfold during Christmastime in Philadelphia, but it was Rated R, which was no-no regarding showing movies in high schools in our state. Had the movie been edited in some way or perhaps been pre-approved by someone in charge, things might have worked out differently, but as is it was, things unfolded in a rather bizarre way.

The day was the Friday before the two-week break. Classes were going along merrily. Some teachers were showing films like *Miracle on 34th Street* and *It's a Wonderful Life* while the substitute for financial lit was showing the R-rated *Trading Places* uncut with all its language and nudity warnings. No one even knew what was happening until a parent called and talked to the principal telling him that her daughter had texted her, complaining of the movie she was watching in her financial lit class.

Things really snowballed from there. Administration was pulling their hair out and exclaiming, "What was the Ebenezer Scrooge was she thinking?"

The principal ran, literally, up three flights of stairs to the classroom in question and immediately turned off the movie, much to the chagrin of some of the male students, but relieving the girl who'd been texting her mom. Rudolph the Red-Nosed Reindeer was put on in its place (not quite a stock market blockbuster), and the substitute was brought down to the main office like a misbehaving student. Had she been a few years younger, we might have called her parents. But as it was, she was excused for the day, and we never saw her as a sub again. Whether because the district didn't use her again or whether because of her embarrassment, we never found out.

Another sub-T that was asked never to return to our school was a young man who spent the entire day on the computer, checking out his mating prospects and fine-tuning his profile on one or two online dating sites and, more surprisingly, posting on an adult chat room.

We used to provide a blanket password for guests to use while in our building, but after he used it for his love connection (and when school was over left all the sites open for the teacher to find the next morning), we did away with that policy. It was a case of the one bad apple spoiling the whole barrel and another sub-T crossed off our list.

We were going through substitutes like they were wet wipes in a nursery. We had subs getting lost in our parking lot (which wasn't very big), subs getting lost on the way to our parking lot because they didn't know which way east was, and subs getting in accidents in our parking. One grandpa came into the main office to report that a substitute tried to run him over. I had my doubts about that one; the others, however, were bona-fide true stories. We even had a substitute get lost in the building, unable to find her way out. We were in serious need of substitutes for our substitutes.

My favorite narrative about any substitute was the story of Mrs. Proctor, an older ex-English-teacher who had been filling in for our science teacher who had been out on maternity leave for several weeks. She was a little hard of hearing and had a bit of arthritis in her fingers, but she was keeping off the dating sites and staying awake in class, so she was doing a pretty good job as subs go.

When the science teacher's maternity leave was extinguished, she decided that she was going to leave her teaching position and be a stay-at-home mom to her new baby girl, and who could blame her? But now we were in need of a science teacher to finish out this school year and possibly come back for the next one.

Since it was the middle of the school year, we did not have many prospects applying for the job. In fact, we had only three candidates to interview. To our surprise, Mrs. Proctor was one of the three. She could be a logical choice. She had already been teaching the class. She knew the curriculum and the kids liked her, so we scheduled her for an interview after school on a Friday afternoon.

Mrs. Proctor came in to her interview with her new hairdo and what looked to be a new outfit. She sat across the conference room table from the interviewing committee, which consisted of the principal, the assistant principal, and a representative from the district. She seemed a little nervous yet confident in a way. She answered each question thoughtfully and thoroughly and touched a bit on her previous teaching experience. Then Ms. Graham asked her about her knowledge of the curriculum, since English, not science, was her certified subject.

"Can you tell us about why you think you are qualified to teach science, Mrs. Proctor?" the principal asked.

"Well," began the aging teacher, "as you know, I have been substitute teaching this class for several weeks now, but what really qualifies me is that every afternoon when I get home, I get on my treadmill and walk for twenty minutes. While I am walking, I watch Bill Nye the Science Guy on the cable channel."

She was very animated and proud of herself. I'm not really sure if she was proud that she could walk twenty minutes or because she was watching Bill Nye. Nevertheless, she was pleased with her accomplishment and continued,

"I have seen every episode twice, and some of them even three times. That really teaches you a lot. I think that qualifies me, don't you?"

Granted it was more experience than some of our sub-Ts had, but not exactly what we had in mind for a full-time teacher. The committee was sure that Mrs. Proctor would not be their choice for science teacher, but the interview continued. To their credit, they did not stop it in the middle and just ask her to leave. Mr. Montgomery was trying to get the interview over with, but Ms. Graham kept asking questions of the lady, and it went on and on. Mr. M tried signaling her to cut it short. He tried kicking her under the table. He was trying not to laugh out loud, but it became too much for him, and he had to leave the room. In fact, the entire committee was struggling keeping their faces straight. She was so cute and earnest. Ms. Graham, also sweet and sincere, concluded the interview with,

"We will take the weekend to consider all the candidates and let you know next week."

Mrs. Proctor seemed thrilled that she was being considered; I don't think she thought she would even be called for an interview. Needless to say, she was not hired for the position, but she remained a capable sub for us. Maybe we just needed to show reruns of Bill Nye the Science Guy in the class to teach the kids.

As anyone in public education knows, there is no substitute for a good substitute. When it comes to substitute teachers, it's always a roll of the dice. There are, of course, wonderful subs who genuinely want to do a good job for the teacher, who are truly interested in the kids and care about the condition of the classroom they leave at the end of the day, and they are the ones you want to hold on to and call on when their services are needed, but there are those who take the job just for the paycheck, and not a very good one at that.

CHAPTER 8

TOO SCHOOL FOR COOL

The snow began falling as I drove to work on a chilly Wednesday morning in January. It put me in a somber mood because I knew that by the time I returned home, I would be shoveling a foot or more of heavy winter snow. I also realized that the snow would mean snowballs, snowball fights, and angry motorists and bus drivers who would be barraged with snowballs by our students; it never failed. The snow could not possibly stay on the ground; it had to be flying in one form or another.

One of the best things about working at the school was that we usually were released from work not long after the kids were released from school, which meant it was still light when I got home, even in the cold winter months when the days were shorter. It was still snowing lightly as I drove toward my house that afternoon, so when I arrived, the first thing I did was start to work on shoveling the driveway and sidewalks around my home.

I put my head down and all my weight behind the shovel as I worked to scrape and remove the ice from the cement walks. I let my mind wander to warm sandy Mexican beaches and rum-laced cocktails as I froze my behind off in the freezing weather. I was languishing in my happy place when *bam!* A snowball hit me square in the shoulder and my dream melted away like Frosty the Snowman in Southern California.

I dropped my snow shovel, and my head snapped up as I searched for the snow-slinging culprit. I did not have to search far. When I raised my head, I saw a car parked by the curb of my house with Mr. Brent Frazier standing beside it. *Bam!* Another frozen snowball hit me in the front of my fluffy parka, and the ice crystals pelted my face.

"Stop that!" I protested and raised my hand to deflect another icy bullet speeding toward my forehead.

Mr. Frazier, history teacher, volleyball coach, and driver's education instructor, stood by the school district vehicle, laughing as I lunged at him with my shovel raised above my head, ready to defend myself.

"Get back in that car and drive away as fast as you can, Brent!" I yelled at him and tried to think of how I was going to get back at him the next day.

He jumped back in the car that was marked "STUDENT DRIVER" on its sides and across the back; he instructed the student to hit the gas. I ran after them for a half a block in my bulky snow boots that were like running on the sand wearing swim fins. Off they went down the street toward the school, and all I could think was, *What is he teaching those kids?*

However, I was not surprised by the cavalier attitude and lack of self-discipline shown by the young teacher. He was always pulling a prank on someone at the school, whether it be staff, teachers, or students; even the administration was not immune to the antics of the practical joker.

I was more than a little annoyed, not only because my friend and colleague had deluged me with snowballs, but because it was snowing even harder now and was covering the walks faster than I could shovel.

As I have said, Mr. Frazier was a mischief-maker. He was a twenty-eight-year-old Dennis the Menace, not too far removed from college and much-loved by the students. Mostly because they were all on the same intellectual level, I suppose. He was hip, rad, trendy, and cool. But he had a few habits as a driver's education teacher that would literally drive the kids and the main office staff absolutely bonkers.

Aside from the mishap with the snowballs, Mr. Frazier took his job teaching the young teenagers to drive pretty seriously. He would never let them have a cell phone in his car or rather the car that was specially made and used as his teaching tool for the school. The driver's ed car was like a normal car, except on the passenger's side where the teacher sat, there was an extra brake in case the student was about to hit a phone pole or drive off the overpass into a skate park, the instructor could stop the car from his side.

Of course, when the kids weren't behind the wheel, they saw it as the perfect time to be on their phones, texting, surfing, or playing games as they sat in the back seat. Mr. Frazier, however, saw it as an insult to his teaching. This from a teacher who stops a driving lesson to throw snowballs at the office secretary as she shovels snow.

"They should be paying attention to what everyone is doing in the car." He would preach. "The driver, the teacher, and the other passengers."

Whenever he would catch a student with a phone in the car while they were out on a drive, he would snatch the phone from perpetrator's hands, roll down his window, and say,

"See that bush?"

White as a bed sheet and scared to death that he was going to throw their phone out the window, the student with the phone, or now without their phone, would slowly nod. Then Mr. Frazier would say,

"That's where your phone is. You can pick it up after school."

Affirming their sheer horror, out the window the phone would sail, and most of the time, it would land in the appointed bush, and the student would be mortified and nearly pass out. Not only was their treasured cell phone gone for who knows how long, but now they were going to have to walk to retrieve it or call Mom or Dad to have them pick up the wayward phone. Can you imagine that call?

"Hey, Mom, my driver's ed teacher threw my phone out the window of the car during our drive today. It's in the bush at the corner of the park and the school. Could you pick it up for me?"

Oh yeah, there were a lot of furious parents when they heard that the brand-new two-hundred-dollar phone they'd just bought for their son or daughter just went out the window, quite literally. It would only take a few of these cordless phone flights and conversations with incensed parents, usually at the first week of a semester, then everyone would get the hint. Don't take your phone on your drive with Mr. Frazier, or at least don't get caught using it.

One sunny afternoon late in the spring, two college-aged students came hurrying into the main office in a panic and wanted to know who they could talk to about someone stealing their cell phone while they were talking on it in the park. One was a petite girl with long black hair, flawless pale skin, and panic in her eyes, and her companion was tall and lanky with straggly dark brown hair and what I can only describe as a look of bewilderment on his face. Both were wearing shorts, T-shirts, and sandals and looked to be students, but not ours. When I inquired as to what happened exactly, because frankly I was a little lost, the young girl spoke very quickly and said,

"I was talking on my phone while we were walking around the park. We were trying to catch up with a few of our friends to eat lunch with them because we all couldn't decide where to go. A man came jogging by and took my phone. He said, 'You know you are not supposed to be in the park during lunch, and you are not supposed to have this. You can pick it up in the main office after school.' Then he grabbed my phone and jogged off. We weren't sure which main office we needed to go to, but then we were like, maybe it's the high school, so here we are. I would like to get my phone back and find out what all of this is about."

She was talking so fast that I was having a hard time keeping up with the dialogue, and I was thinking that I would like to find out what this was all about, too, because I certainly didn't have a clue, nor did I have a phone to give her. I opened a drawer behind the counter and pulled out an incident report form to take down the information I needed to solve this mystery. I noticed that we only had one or two forms left—meaning, we had filled out a lot of reports on skirmishes and such, signaling that we'd had a lot of incidents.

That's not good, I thought, making a mental note to copy more incident forms.

Then I led the victim and her tall witness to the conference room, where we could all sit down to discuss, deliberate, and decide what to do next. My inner secretary removed her secretary hat and carefully set it aside where it would not get crumpled, and my inner detective reached for her Sherlock Holmes detective cap and put it squarely on her head to begin the interrogation.

"You are not students here, right?" I began.

They both shook their heads. Negative.

"We both go to the community college," the young lady said. This made sense because both schools were close to the park being discussed.

"What did the guy who took your phone look like?" I asked.

"A jogger," replied the young man with the disheveled hair. It seemed to him to be a perfectly reasonable description. I stared at him for a minute, wondering what his major at college might be. Then I looked back and forth between them for a second. This was going to be harder than I thought. I was going to have to hold their hands and lead them on this journey of discovery that we were about to take.

"Can you describe him?" I ventured, afraid of what the answer might be.

"This dude was just too school for cool." I flinched inwardly at his reply, but it was my fault for asking, I guess.

I turned to the young woman for help. She returned my look with an expectant gaze.

"How tall was he?" I prompted.

"Like five eleven or five twelve." I actually wrote on the form, "Like 5 feet 12 inches." It was the only thing I'd written down so far. Then I added, "Students from the community college."

I was considering asking how fast the jogger was running but decided against it. I was developing a theory about what had happened, and I had a suspicion of who the culprit might be, but all I had right now was circumstantial evidence and nothing really concrete.

"He was dressed in, like, biking stuff," she offered.

"Uh-huh," I said as I gave my best Joe Friday from *Dragnet* impersonation, resisting the urge to say, "Just the facts, ma'am." Instead I asked, "Hair color?"

"Longish blond."

I wondered if this was a new blond shade or if she were giving me the color and the length all in one description. The evidence against my suspect was piling up. I pushed the form toward them across the table and asked the woman to write down exactly what happened and everything she could remember.

"I will need your signature on the bottom," I instructed. "I'll be right back," I told them as I left the room to make a quick phone call. I looked at the clock and noted that the bell was about to ring for passing between classes. I pick up the receiver and dialed the history classroom.

"Yeah?" Mr. Frazier's voice came over the line.

I jumped right in, "Brent, did you confiscate a phone in the park today at lunch?"

"Yeah," he said. "Two kids. I told them they could come after school to pick it up. I'll have it down to you before the end of the day."

"Well," I began, "those two kids aren't ours. They are students down at the community college."

"No kidding," he said and began laughing. One thing you could always count on was Brent Frazer cracking himself up. "They looked just like our kids."

"Maybe you should bring that phone down now and apologize to these two," I suggested with no mirth in my voice.

His voice took on a more serious I-might-be-in-trouble tone. "Yeah, right," he said and hung up the phone.

I returned to the conference room where my victim and witness seemed to be struggling to fill out the incident report. All she needed to do was write down some details, but the page was still nearly blank.

"I found your phone," I informed them.

The girl actually squealed and shot up from her chair. She clapped her hands together and jumped up and down.

"Yeah!" she yelled excitedly.

"Cool," her companion said. "Who *was* that dude?"

"One of our teachers who runs in the park at lunch," I said.

"How did you figure it out?" he asked.

They both looked at me like I'd just solved the most thrilling mystery ever.

"Well," I said, my subconscious leveling her detective's hat, "we only have one teacher that does that, and he fit the description you gave me."

"Cool," he said again.

Just then a student came running in with the phone in his hand. He gave it to me, and there was a sticky note attached to it with a single word scrawled on it. *Sorry* was scribbled on the tiny piece of paper. It looked like it had been written by a second grader. I guess there would be no formal apologies. The young woman rolled her eyes, and the guy said,

"Maybe someone should take his phone while he is running in the park."

Or throw it out the window of the driver's ed car, I thought to myself.

You will probably not be surprised to learn that Mr. Frazier did not make it as a teacher very long. When we returned to school after summer vacation that year, there was a new teacher in his place for all his classes—history, volleyball, and driver's education. Rumors flew around the teacher's lounge about what had become of him.

As we all found out later, over the course of the summer, Mr. Frazier had been "borrowing" the special driver's ed car with the extra brake on the wrong side and had been giving private lessons while school was not in session.

While everyone else was going on vacation, splashing in the pools around the city, hanging out with friends, and doing all the summer things that happen during June, July, and August, Brent was cutting the principal's signature off old driver's ed certificates and placing them on new ones, then copying them on the Xerox machine in the office, sort of the original cut-and-paste job. Then he would give them out to the drivers he was illegally training and turning them loose on the unsuspecting commuters.

Well, I never said he wasn't resourceful.

Following that well-spent hour and five minutes figuring out Brent's latest escapade, a call came into the office. I answered, wondering, *What now?*

"Hello," A pleasant voice said from the receiver. "My name is Marely Hansen, and I was just wondering if my car is ready?"

"I'm afraid you have me at a loss," I confessed. "What was supposed to happen with your car?"

"Well," she began, "I dropped it off outside your auto shop doors last night to be fixed, and I wondered if it was done and when I could pick it up."

What, did we change our name to Quick Lube overnight and no one told me? Apparently, she'd heard from a mom or two around the neighborhood that their son or daughter had been taking auto shop classes and they'd had their oil changed or tires rotated by the students for practice at no charge. So she figured if she left the car outside the garage doors in back of the school that were the entrance to the auto shop with a note explaining the problem, they would get right to it and have it fixed in a jiffy, and she wouldn't have to pay a mechanic.

"Do you have a student attending school here?" I asked.

She hesitated and said, "No, but I figured they could practice on my car because it hasn't been running well lately."

Oh. There are a couple of things wrong with this theory. First, we are not an all-service car center where you can drop your car off and have the students or, more likely, the instructor fix it. Second, we've had a couple of mishaps with cars that have had minor repairs. Not the least of which was a tire falling off after the lug nuts weren't properly tightened. I wanted to ask, "Are you sure you want the students working on your car?" Instead, I explained that only cars of students or parents were eligible to have their lug nuts worked on and only after a waiver was signed and approved.

"There is just too much liability and too many things that can go wrong," I said.

"Oh, I would never complain about any work that was done," she insisted.

Easy to say unless you are driving on three wheels.

CHAPTER 9

GO SELL CRAZY
SOMEWHERE ELSE

The school district was always considered a "good job" in our community as it was in probably every community across the nation. The pay wasn't always the highest, but the benefits were highly sought after. The hours were good, the time off was great, and the working conditions were tolerable if you liked children and lots of 'em.

When positions came available, they usually didn't last long. There were always numerous applicants ready, or so they thought, for the trials of middle school life. Usually, we didn't have many jobs available during the year, but there was one particular year when we were short at every turn. We had several people quit midyear, and we had a devil of a time replacing them. We needed a variety of people, from floor sweeping specialists to trigonometry teachers.

We were conducting interviews almost daily during this time, which only added to the mayhem that we called the main office, and it sort of made every day feel like Monday. We were in search of an office clerk for the front desk, a position that we had filled with many competent women from our community who had children who had either attended or were currently attending our school. Like these other times, we had a lady named Marion apply for the position whose daughter was in the seventh grade, a lovely girl named Belle.

The afternoon that Marion came in for her interview was an especially busy one. The phones were ringing, a few parents had come in to take their children home a little early, as they often did, and her interview was scheduled for a few minutes after the last bell rang. She was early, always a good idea when interviewing, and she was friendly and chatted with the secretaries and office aides until the bell sounded and it was time for the school day to end. When the bell rang, the chaos increased exponentially, and the interviewee left the front counter and sat at a nearby desk where we took care of new registrations.

We kept a laptop arranged on the desk with a number of forms, pens, and pamphlets proclaiming the accolades of our school. While she awaited her time with the administration, she read the forms, thumbed through a pamphlet or two, then she proceeded to unplug the laptop, wind the cord into a neat bundle and drop it into the large purse she was carrying.

Just as I came hurrying around the corner to show her into the conference room for her interview, she was picking up the laptop and stuffing that into her purse as well. She looked up and saw me staring at her and said,

"Oh! I thought this laptop was mine. It looks just like mine."

"No," I replied incredulously, more than slightly taken aback. "We keep *our* computer on this desk so it's there when we need it for registration."

"Well, do you need it now?" she asked.

I guess you don't just leave your registration laptop out on the desk if you don't want someone to walk away with it. Just like at Red Lobster, you don't leave lobsters in the tank in the lobby if you don't want some crazy person running in and grabbing one, then running out the front door with it. Now, if they took the rubber bands off their front claws, things like that wouldn't happen, and if we had giant claws on our laptops, it probably wouldn't have happened to us either.

"Could you just put it back on the desk?" I asked with a little more edge to my voice than I would have liked. "Please?" I added.

The gal took our computer out of her bag and placed it back on the table, acting as if nothing out of the ordinary had just happened. She also retrieved the cord from her purse and plugged everything in as it was before. She straightened the forms and pamphlets, then she plucked a tissue from the box on the corner of the desk and wiped everything down. Afterward, she turned on her heel and walked out the office door. I guess she either forgot all about her interview, or she figured that since she'd just tried to make off with our laptop, she probably wasn't going to be hired for the job anyway.

I stepped into the conference room to relay the story of the lady who was here for an interview, tried to steal our computer, then left.

"So there won't be an interview today," I told the interviewing committee. "Unless you want to call the police and have them over to interview us about the whole thing."

We decided against filing a complaint against Marion. As we all exited the room, the same woman was coming back through the door.

"Uh-oh," I said aloud, giving my best Bill Walton impression. "This can't be good."

"I locked my keys in the car," she announced. "Is there anyone here who can give me a ride to the train station?" she asked. "I think I have a spare set at home, but I live way up north, and it takes a good hour to get there from here."

Now, the fact that this woman had just tried to apprehend our laptop from the main office notwithstanding, none of us were really jumping at the chance to give her a ride anywhere, let alone the train station, which was probably a good twenty miles away from where we were. Someone spoke up,

"Maybe you should call home first to find out for sure if you have a spare before you go all the way there."

"Oh no!" she protested. "I could never do that. I live with my parents, and my dad likes to have a few cocktails in the afternoon, and I don't think he would ever be able to find them. I'll just go outside and break a window," she said and did an about-face to return to her car and smash the window. We stared in her wake, and I ran after her to bring her back into the main office.

"Maybe we should try something a little less drastic first," I suggested.

"Maybe you're right," she agreed. "I'd hate to hurt myself breaking the glass."

Not to mention the difficulty replacing the window. By this time, the congestion in the office had subsided, and her daughter, Belle, had joined us.

"Why don't we try a coat hanger?" Belle asked, and I thought, *She's been watching too many TV shows where this trick was used to heist a car.*

"That's a great idea!" her mom replied before I had a chance to object.

Seriously?

I began to wonder if Dad was the only one who perhaps had a few cocktails that afternoon. Nonetheless, we proceeded to locate a metal coat hanger, which was not easy given all the plastic alternatives available, but we found one, and after several minutes of bending and pulling, we'd straightened it out as much as we could. Then all of us still present marched out to the parking lot to attempt to gain access to the car in question like a gang of thugs getting ready to steal a car stereo.

We would not have made very good thieves. We all gave it a try, and we all failed. Turns out breaking into a car with a hanger isn't quite as easy as they make it out on *Law and Order*. I might add here that neither is opening a locked door with a credit card. Don't ask me how I know.

Back to the breaking and entering in progress.

After we had all had a turn with the hanger—and by *all* I mean the able-bodied principal, the above-average-intelligence assistant principal, me (the more-than-capable secretary), the somewhat-skilled custodian with his trusty tools, and the questionably competent woman who owed the car in the first place—her thirteen-year-old daughter, Belle, asked,

"Can I try?"

Hmmm, my inner detective was suspicious as we watched her take the coat hanger, use a screwdriver to create an ample space to slip the metal rod between the door and the body of the car, snag the lock to give it a tug, and open it.

To everyone's amazement, she opened the lock in matter of seconds, just like she'd done it before. Hmmm, again. I raised my eyebrows and was just about to ask if she had any other criminal skills or experience, but her elated mother gave an excited squeal and jumped into the car, found the keys, and started the ignition. She rolled down the window, and I thought she was going to thank us for helping even though we had done very little in the way of assistance. Instead she asked,

"So did I get the job?"

Could it be she thought this was a test? Maybe she thought this was part of the interview. My subconscious shrugged and shook her head in disbelief. Our principal, Ms. Graham replied, "No. I don't think we will be needing your services."

"Okay," the woman said with a smile and a wave, and she was off onto her next adventure. I could only imagine what that would be, but she had her capable daughter, Belle, with all of her abilities in the front seat with her, so I figured she was in good hands.

Mr. Montgomery, the assistant principal, said, as we watched her drive off, "I think we should have hired her for the entertainment value. We could pop some popcorn, sit back, and watch the show!"

We all had a good laugh and thanked our lucky stars that she hadn't somehow made it past the interviewing process and ended up at our front desk. I could only imagine the circus that would be six hundred teenagers *and* Marion at the counter. That would be like Dustin Hoffman as *Rain Man* trying to navigate a bus through LA rush-hour traffic.

"No way! I don't care how much popcorn there is. That show just wouldn't be worth it," Ms. Graham quickly responded, and we all laughed again, wondering how that woman had made it this far in life left to her own devices.

The one thing you should never ask when working in the main office of a public middle school is "What could possibly to wrong?"

If you do, you will always find out, usually sooner rather than later.

Mr. Montgomery, our fearless assistant principal, was in the habit of asking this very dangerous question first thing every morning. I think the reasoning behind this was that you might as well get it over with early in the day and not have any surprises later.

While posing his question, he would always whistle Julius Fucik's "Entrance of the Gladiators," better known as the circus theme song. Every time I heard Mr. M whistling that tune, I would think of twenty clowns popping out of a bright-yellow polka-dotted VW bug or twenty junior high students popping out of a bathroom stall, almost the same thing.

Things go wrong. That's just how it is in a public school. It's like a petri dish for things to go wrong. When things start to head south, it's best to remember a few key elements. First, it could be worse. Please refer to Marty Feldman and Gene Wilder digging up a body in *Young Frankenstein*. Second, it can't last forever. When things go sideways, they will eventually straighten out and get back on track. Lastly, next week, it won't even matter because something new will go astray. If the office is out of control, the best thing you can do is buckle up and brace for the impact. This, too, shall pass.

You might think that with a building full of twelve and thirteen-year old children, they would be the cause of most of the breakdowns that occur, and they certainly had their share of collapses; however, a large percent of the hiccups in the well-oiled, smooth-running machine that was our main office occurred due to the parent factor, that unpredictable element that could throw the most sophisticated jet into a ferocious tailspin.

Take Heidi for instance. She was a cute little seventh grader, new to the world of junior high school but seemingly stable. She reminded me of the girl in the Disney movie Heidi. Not only because she had the same name but also because she had long, thick blond braids, and round rosy cheeks. She was as meek and mild as Dorothy from *The Wizard of Oz* and desperately wanted to please her teachers. I could see her killing the wicked witch with a bucket of water and then apologizing for it.

Heidi came into the office one day, leaned far over my desk like she was going to tell me a secret, and asked in a quiet voice if she could talk to me alone. The first thing that came to me was she might need some feminine supplies. This was how most of the girls approached me when they did, but Heidi did not. Instead she asked, "Do you have a couple of sticky notepads that I could have?"

So she wanted pads, just not the kind I thought. It was an odd request, and I couldn't help but ask her why she needed them.

"I need them to help me remember to go to the bathroom," she stated succinctly.

I considered the possibilities and the implications of this statement. I wasn't sure I wanted to know why, but I was now very curious.

"I don't understand," I said carefully.

"Well, sometimes I forget" was her shy and simple answer, her blue eyes looking directly at me, waiting for my response.

It occurred to me that she'd probably been potty trained for a good ten or eleven years. It also occurred to me that this conversation wasn't going to be easy. I took a deep cleansing breath and pried a little more.

"How can you forget to go to the bathroom, Heidi?" I probed.

She looked a little embarrassed, and I thought that maybe I shouldn't have asked her. Then she said something that I couldn't believe.

"Well, I really don't forget," she confessed. "I remind myself to go because I am afraid of the toilet, and sometimes I wait too long, then I have an accident and have to call my dad to bring me new clothes to change into. It's scary, all that whooshing water and loud noise." It was now her turn to take a deep breath. Then she continued, "My dad and my brother have the same problem."

I was stunned and powerless to speak. Even if I could have, I didn't know what to say to her. I'd never had a student or a parent afraid of the toilet before, and I was having a hard time wrapping my mind around the circumstances. I gained my composure and said, "Well, we don't want that, do we?"

She shyly shook her head and seemed relieved that I understood her predicament, which I really didn't, but sometimes you just need to fake it. I took her back to my desk and gave her the sticky notes she'd requested. After she'd left the office, I talked to our counselor about the situation and hoped that she might meet with her and her dad and somehow resolve the problem.

Teachers I know have described parents as unpredictable, spontaneous, stubborn, unstable, deranged, maddening, and obsessive-compulsive. I have known parents that are all these. But then you get the parent that is just flat-out squirrel-chasin' nuts.

One such mom was Mrs. Maria Roland, mother of Ann, a somewhat flighty girl with long dark-brown hair and large brown eyes. Mrs. Roland was a bit older than most of our parents. She was in the 45–47 age group. She was a small Hispanic woman who stood about four feet ten inches. She had short curly hair, very round cheeks, and a double chin. She had a permanent furrow between her eyebrows which made her look perpetually angry. Probably because she *was* perpetually angry—at least it seemed that way.

She would call the main office a couple of times a day for various reasons. Sometimes she'd call to make sure her daughter, Ann, made it to school on the bus all right even though we hadn't lost a child on the bus yet. She'd call to find out what time we'd be releasing the kids even though we released them at the same time every day. She called to check when spring break was even though it was only September. I was convinced she would call because she didn't have anything else to do and just wanted to see if someone would actually answer the phone, and if no one answered the phone, she would become terribly agitated and keep calling until someone finally did.

One particular Thursday morning when the main office was as hectic as the neighborhood Walmart on Black Friday, she called to find out if it was going to be possible for her daughter to be in the school musical and still participate in the afterschool sports program that was offered.

I explained to her, "That would be difficult, Mrs. Roland, since play practice is after school at the same time as the sports practices are scheduled. I don't think she will be able to do both, but I will talk to Mr. Horace, the play director, to see if it might work out."

She was very pleasant, which was out of character for her, and asked if I could please let her know what I found out by lunchtime. I told her that I would call her back to let her know as soon as I talked with Mr. Horace, which, in fact, I did. However, after my conference with the director, I called Mrs. Roland, but she did not answer. I called again a few minutes later and tried again after the third period bell. I must have called her five or six times without reaching her, and I was unable to leave her a message as her voice mailbox was not set up.

Lunchtime was quickly approaching, and the kids would be filling the cafeteria very soon. I tried to reach her one more time with no success. Shortly thereafter, I saw Ann eating her lunch in the, cafeteria and I quickly walked out to mention to her that I spoke with Mr. Horace, and he said it would be too grueling for her to do both—the musical practices and the sporting program on top of memorizing lines and keeping up with homework. He just didn't see how it could work.

"Let your mom know that I talked to Mr. Horace and he said you will have to choose between the two," I told her. "It's either the play or soccer."

"Okay," she said, not really paying attention or seeming too disappointed or interested one way or the other.

Her mother, on the other hand, was livid. Not because Ann couldn't participate in both activities but because I had talked to her about making the choice. Just before three o'clock that afternoon, Mrs. Roland came storming into the office with the wrath of the Almighty following her.

"You had no right to talk with Ann about the play!" she screeched before she even reached my desk. "That was between me and my daughter. You didn't have to get involved."

There are times when life in the main office is like backing up a boat at the marina. Once it starts going bad, there is no fixing it. Next thing you know, you're off the dock and sunk. This felt like one of those times. I quickly pointed out to Mrs. Roland, in self-defense, that she had been the person who involved me.

"You called me and asked me to talk to the play director to see what I could find out," I reminded her. "I could not reach you after we talked, so I relayed the message to Ann."

"You can't talk to me like that!" she yelled. "You didn't do me any favors."

Sometimes you're the dog; sometimes you're the hydrant.

Ms. Graham came running out of her office upon hearing raised voices. She tried to calm the woman down, as I was completely at a loss here, but Mrs. Roland was inconsolable. I stood looking at her, watching her chins bounce up and down as she raved and ranted and cussed me out. Mrs. Graham, who stood five-nine, led the smaller woman out of the office to discuss and diffuse the situation. They chatted animatedly for a bit; Mrs. Roland kept pointing at me through the glass and staring emphatically with a look that did not say we were going to be the best of friends.

After a bit, the principal came back to the office, and the irate mother was left sitting on the steps a few feet from the office door, talking to herself, and from the looks of it, having quite a lengthy conversation.

"Are you all right?" Mrs. G asked, and I nodded.

"Can you speak?" she broke into a contagious smile.

"Yes," I answered with the corners of my mouth lifting, "but I am afraid of what I might say if I do."

She asked for my side of the story, which I gave her.

"Why don't you leave a few minutes early today?" she offered.

I looked out of the office and saw Mrs. Roland sitting on the stairs right outside the door, then I looked back at my boss. This time, I shook my head, wondering how long she was going to sit there and stew about the incident. Eventually, I was going to have to walk past her to leave the school and go to my car. I am not ashamed to admit I was a little nervous about another confrontation.

Mrs. Graham returned to her office, and I returned to my desk. There was a half an hour left until the end of my day. I kept one eye on the distraught mother and the other one on my computer. I was starting to become a bit cross-eyed when about fifteen minutes later she walked back into the office. I stiffened at her approach, but I looked her right in the eye as she came closer to the desk.

"I have a couple of light bulbs out at my house," she began, "and I was wondering if you had any extras." She asked this as if I were her next-door neighbor, and she was asking to borrow a cup of sugar. There was no mention of the previous outburst and no hint at any kind of apology or angst.

I just stared at her trying not to let my mouth drop open. I wasn't sure what I was expecting when she entered my office, but this certainly was not it.

"N-n-n-no," I stammered. "I don't think I do."

"Okay," she said, and then she paused for a moment or two. With her index finger on her chin, she looked up at the ceiling as if in great thought and then she asked, "What about paper plates?"

I blinked at her a couple of times and looked around to see if anyone else was witnessing the situation and if I'd heard her correctly. No one was available to help me or confirm her request, so I turned and left my desk without a word. I walked back to our break room, returned with a small stack of paper plates, and handed them to her.

Finally appeased, Mrs. Roland left the office and the building with her paper plates in hand. I just stood there, silent, watching her go. All I could think of was Jack Nicholson in *As Good As It Gets* when his character Melvin Udall exclaims as only he can, "Go sell crazy somewhere else. We're all full up here."

I have been lucky enough in my life to have only interviewed for four big-girl jobs besides the part-time jobs I'd held in high school. When they asked the inevitable question about how I dealt with difficult people, I always told the story of Mrs. Roland and her paper plates and her daughter who eventually took a part in the school play and then quit two weeks later to play soccer.

Part Three

Animals at Large

CHAPTER 10

BEVERLY WITH THE
FRIENDLY EYES

Many science teachers are born animal lovers, especially the ones with backgrounds in biology. As a whole, I have observed that biology teachers love what they teach about, as most teachers do if they are any good. As such, a few of our animal-loving biology teachers kept animals in their classrooms for their students to observe, care-for, learn from, and report on.

One of my favorite teachers was a biology teacher named Mr. Johnson, whom the students deemed Dr. J because he always wore a white lab coat when he was teaching and because Julius (Dr. J) Irving was at the height of his basketball career. He was partly bald, always wore glasses on the end of his nose, and if you saw him on the street you would probably say to yourself, "I bet that guy is a biology teacher."

My children were students of his, and he was awesome at his job. Upon his retirement, he said that he had lived his dream life. All he had ever wanted his whole life was to have a large family and to be a biology teacher.

"I know it sounds corny," he confessed, "but it's true."

He got both of his wishes, and he won the district's Teacher of the Year award twice. Dr. J was very smart with a great sense of humor. He once told me that he liked to keep as many animals as possible at school, because his wife would only let him have one pet, a golden retriever named Sheila, at home.

And keep them he did. Between him and the other two biology teachers in our school, they had a veritable petting zoo. They had everything from bunny rabbits to iguanas. Goldfish, hamsters, frogs, birds, snakes, mice, and several other creeping and crawly creatures adorned the classrooms in the science wing of the school. Also, persevered animals like mounted lizards were displayed on painted Styrofoam rocks, portrayed in candid, life-like actions, and stuffed birds flew from the hanging florescent lights in his room. Dr. J had enough ferns, philodendrons, and other potted plants to turn his room into a not-so-endangered rain forest.

The students would water the plants—in most cases, overwater them. They would also care for the animals. Clean the cages, feed them, play with them and love them every day. When summer arrived, some students were allowed to take the various animals home to care for them until school began again in the fall. The teachers just hoped that there were actually kids that would sign up, then follow through and return in September with the animal having survived the summer.

Then they would settle into their new school-year routines, new classrooms and new cages, both the students and the animals, and embark on an exciting new time—nine months full of adventure. Or at least that's what we hope for the first few days, then it was school as usual, same homework, same announcements, blah, blah, blah. Though we did have one administrator who was partial to making our daily announcements in different voices every day. So that was something to look forward to each morning.

However, early one October, students were well into their year, as were the teaches and the office staff, when we received an e-mail on a Monday morning from one of our female biology teachers that was totally out of the norm. It read: "Good Monday morning, all. I arrived at school today only to find that my female tarantula has escaped her enclosure in the science wing. I have been looking for her everywhere and have been unable to locate her. She is brown and fury and very gentle. Her name is Beverly, and she has very friendly eyes, so you will know her if you see her. If you find her, please don't step on her or kill her. Call me, and I will come to rescue her; she is probably very afraid."

She is very afraid? Okay then. Everyone was quite taken aback, and no one was sure what to think or how to react to the news that a huge spider was on the loose and at large in the school and no one knew where she was. This news, which spread like a wildfire in July through the staff, as well as the student body, was met with more than a little anxiety. At first, there was some mild panic and more than a few bad jokes.

"If there is fur where your hamster used to be, report a Beverly sighting."

"If you see a large tarantula, try to get a good look at her eyes to see if she is friendly."

"Beware of Beverly" could be heard all around the school. Signs were posted outside classrooms that read:

> LOST: VERY LARGE SPIDER WITH FRIENDLY EYES
> ANSWERS TO THE NAME OF BEVERLY
> WANTED: ALIVE

No reward was posted; nonetheless, after a few days, the buzz died down, and nearly two weeks later, Beverly hardly entered anybody's conversation. However, there were some members of the custodial staff who reported seeing fewer mice than usual around the building. I am not sure what we expected. Tarantulas do not spin webs to catch their prey, so there would be no looming, creepy spider webs around (no more than usual, anyway) to indicate that Beverly had been there. Yet she remained on the lam, lost in the mayhem of school.

School starts for some districts in late August and for others in early September. After school starts, fall parent-teacher conferences quickly follow and then the downhill slide into the holidays. Halloween is first, although this is much more exciting for the elementary kids. It's still fun for the middle school students, and the high schoolers are still somewhat into the spooky holiday; it's a chance for them to be silly and immature. For big kids, like my husband, Jeff, the fun part of Halloween is handing out candy to the neighborhood kids who dress up and come to ring our doorbell or, in his case, making them do a trick for their treat. However, we always had a lion's share of trick-or-treaters because he would always give out the most popular candy and full-sized not-fun-sized bars.

Halloween at our school meant not only the onset of autumn and the fun of the holiday but also our annual fundraiser, Haunted Hallways. Haunted Hallways was a spook alley of sorts aimed at collecting food for the local food bank for Thanksgiving and Christmas. It happened every year on the Monday night before Halloween. After school, the student body officers would begin decorating for the event. Yards and yards of black plastic-covered walls, lockers, tables, room dividers, and anything else the kids could think to envelop.

Since the theme was a haunted school, teachers were recruited to be ghostly spirits of departed teachers come back to wreak havoc the hallways and classrooms of the school where they once taught. Costumed adults would jump out to startle the adolescents and scare the pants off the student body and their families.

A long-dead science teacher in a bloody lab coat and a dusty laboratory filled with cobwebs boiled toxic potions and poisons (lime green Gatorade) in bubbling beakers. An ancient librarian roamed the stacks of the library bemoaning the beloved books she could no longer read and reach out at the unsuspecting visitors who navigated the maze of bookshelves in the dark with a spattering of lights flashing like lightning revealing other ghosts and goblins in the room.

A specter band teacher led a quartet of skeletal musicians in an ominous opus while brave youngsters were led through a maze of tables in a dark cafeteria where body parts on plates moved around tabletops with rats chasing them. If a guest reached out, a strobe light would flash, and a horrific alarm was set off, sending noise up through the stairwells like smoke up a chimney. It was all very chilling and scary.

In short, Haunted Hallways was a torture chamber of ghoulish teachers and evil educators who created a wicked walk of horror and terror all in the name of fundraising. By the end of the night, we would have three thousand cans of food to sort, box, and deliver to the food bank. It was three years before we got more smarter and charged $1 for each time a guest walked through the spook alley, then we just donated the money at the end instead of packing up cases of canned goods.

In the main office, Halloween was approaching, and during the week before a holiday, any holiday, we liked to decorate the office and let the kids put up some stuff to celebrate the occasion. We decorated for everything, from Christmas to Ground Hog Day, and Halloween was no different. We didn't go all out and wear elaborate costumes because we were already disguised as responsible adults and, as such, we would stick to the tame, boring decorations, but we did make the effort.

Each year, we would build a miniature haunted village with ceramic haunted-looking houses, dead trees, and a graveyard with tiny headstones. It came complete with little ghosts and trick-or-treaters all placed on burlap and accessorized with real fall leaves from my yard. By the time it was all set up, it was quite macabre. Students, teachers, and parents alike would all stop by for a look-see and comment on the tiny haunted town.

One day, just before all Hallows' Eve, our longtime registrar, Cami, came walking briskly into the main office and whooshed by the spooky pocket-sized village. She briefly stopped to check out the ghosts in the cemetery when she noticed a new addition that she hadn't seen before. It was a large spider on the main street poised just behind some unsuspecting goblins, preparing to ambush them. She smiled at the lifelike creature and put her hand out to touch it because it looked so real. Suddenly, it moved in response to her finger coming toward it. She jumped back a bit, startled, but thought the office personnel quite clever for placing a battery-operated spider where it would shock people the most. Then the horrible arachnid began walking down the street, its long legs knocking over small children and trees; even houses and churches were not safe. She then raised up on her long hind legs as real tarantulas often do when threatened.

Cami was a small woman of five-three and just about 125 pounds. She was very sweet, well put together, and always had every hair in place. She was about to turn forty-five years old and had worked at the school district as long as I had. In fact, we started at the same school in the same year. When she saw the spectacle, she jumped back in horror with a screech, and her perfectly coiffed hair fell loose over her forehead. As the large spider began to make her way down the main street, Cami covered her mouth, stumbling backward and pointing at the tiny town.

The office staff looked at her in bewilderment, wondering what could have caused her reaction. Their thoughts were "The small town was haunted, and they tried to make it realistic, but it wasn't *that* scary."

They came to her rescue and quickly discovered that Cami had actually found Beverly, the missing tarantula, although the "friendly eyes" were still in question because no one wanted to get close enough to confirm that was true. But we all assumed it was the long-lost spider that had been the brunt of so many bad jokes and that we'd all forgotten about.

I don't know how much you know about tarantulas, but let me give you a quick tutorial on them: First of all, there are nine hundred different varieties of tarantulas. They are the world's largest spider, and they jump. However, they are actually some of the least aggressive spiders in the arachnid class. Females can live up to thirty years and reach up to eleven inches in length from toe to toe, and they can jump up to the length of their body.

Our Beverly was only about four and a half inches, which means she could potentially jump four and a half inches. Good thing she has friendly eyes because most tarantulas look pretty scary. Despite their fearsome appearance, tarantulas are not threatening to humans even though they jump. Although their bite is venomous, it is no more so than the sting of a honeybee. So it's uncomfortable but not life-threatening. They eat other spiders, beetles, crickets, and small mice among other tarantula delicacies. They catch these by ambushing them (jumping on them) at night. Did I mention that they jump?

After Cami found the wayward spider, the office was all abuzz. I quickly called the science teacher that had originally misplaced the menacing creature; however, she had a substitute filling in for her that day, so I called the science department chair, Dr. J. I explained the situation, and he quickly stated.

"I'll be right down." Then he added, "I have all the equipment we need to catch her."

At that moment, I was wondering what spider-catching equipment looked like and where the store might be to purchase it.

A few long minutes later, we heard his footsteps as he ran down the stairs in front of the office doors two at a time. We had Cami resting comfortably in a chair, recovering with a paper cup full of water, and more than a few students had gathered around the village, observing Beverly's destruction. Dr. J came rushing in with his "equipment," which turned out to be a plastic water pitcher and a good-sized fish net.

"Watch out!" he warned. "Tarantulas tend to jump when they are startled."

See? I told you they jumped. This made a few of the students take a big step back, while there were others who inched a little closer with their cell phones out and at the ready to get a good picture of the beast. One boy was getting so close that I grabbed his shirt and pulled him backward.

"You heard the man, they jump!" I reminded him.

The tarantula was agitated and began running a bit faster instead of just meandering through the town. Then she jumped forward! Everyone standing around watching jumped too. A few cell phones were dropped, and a few screeches were heard, although that could be because the cell phones were dropped. At that very second, Dr. J's giant fish net came crashing down around Beverly, capturing her and making no allowances for escape. It covered her entire body except her long hairy legs, which were still trying to run as she struggled to free herself from the annoying mesh trap. In a flash Dr. J flicked his wrist, and the captured spider was tipped upside down in the net and dropped into the plastic pitcher. Once she was scooped up and safely in the container, many of the students came closer to get a good look while others wisely decided not to venture forward. You never know if she might try to jump out of the receptacle.

It was not unlike the 1958 B-film *Earth vs. the Spider*, where teenagers from a rural community and their high school science teacher join forces to battle a giant mutant spider. No, really, this was really a movie! The similarities were amusing. They were a high school, and we were a high school. They had a janitor, just like our janitor, except our janitor's name wasn't Hugo. Their science teacher tried to come to the rescue; our science teacher *did* come to the rescue. The spider in the movie lived in a huge cave, right outside of town and was awakened by a loud rock band practicing in a garage. We weren't sure where our spider had been living or what had brought her out of hiding and into our small haunted village, but ultimately, the movie spider was captured in the school gymnasium. I was so happy that this was not how our story had ended.

After nearly an hour of chaos, Beverly's reign of tarantula terror was over. The town survived with only one casualty, a miniature trick-or-treater dressed as a pirate, and only one broken lamppost. Cami was quite harried after the attack, and she didn't have every hair still in place, but she looked suitable for work and was mostly fine. The office with all its personnel also survived.

Beverly, with the friendly eyes, was back in her terrarium with her rocks to climb on and the lid secured nice and tight, although there were no more mice to chase. Our Halloween decorations had never been so lively and lifelike, and they would never be that exciting again. However, Cami did have a great story to tell at Thanksgiving dinners for years to come.

CHAPTER 11

MONTY THE PYTHON

I am sure you have heard the saying "The three best things about being a teacher are June, July, and August." It is a common joke among educators. Summer break is a time of joy and relief for students and teachers, especially teachers. It follows that fall break, winter break, and spring break have the same effect.

With all the federal holidays where schools are dismissed, educators average at least one three-day weekend or day off of some kind each month. If it sometimes seems that your children are out of school more than they are in, that is why. There is one month that is an exception to this—March. There is not one federal holiday or extra day off in the month of March, which makes it the longest, grueling month of the school year for everyone involved.

To counter that, the school district built in a day off during March in the form of parent-teacher conferences. They are held twice yearly, midway through the first quarter of the school year and again midway through the third quarter. So autumn and spring, October and March. Although both beautiful times of the year, they can be a bit stressful at school. You might ask, "How does this provide an extra day off?"

I would answer, "PTCs are held in the evening to provide an opportunity for parents to come in to the school to visit with teachers after work. Because the teachers work extra-long hours on these occasions, the district gives them the Friday after PTC off."

Parent-teacher conference time is a period during the school year that generally strikes fear in the hearts of most of the student body, as well as in their parents. Teachers are not immune to the anxiety that accompanies PTCs either because they must prepare for whiny students who may be failing and don't want their parents to know or combative parents whose children may be failing and they blame it on the teacher. After all, they are supposed to be teaching Junior history, and if he doesn't learn it, the teacher must be incompetent.

Even the good students experience some trepidation and anxiety when it comes to parent-teacher conferences. Generally speaking, all the parents who have straight-A students come to PTCs. They spend about three minutes with their darlings' teachers, just enough time to hear how wonderful they are and they are destined for great things. Then they return home, knowing that all is right with the world, or at least their world.

The students who are really struggling or some who have no chance whatsoever of a passing grade that quarter usually lack representation when it comes to PTCs. The middle group have parents that come, if they are informed by their student that its PTC time and if they don't have a good excuse not to attend.

There was a particular autumn when that excuse was provided and the anxiety among students and parents reached new levels. Both groups were already uneasy about PTC, not only because of what the teachers might have to say but also because the week before the conferences were scheduled a large python snake escaped from its aquarium in the science wing of the building and now it was at large somewhere in the bowels of the school.

There are only seven different species of pythons, unlike tarantulas, and they are native to Asia and Africa; however, they are an invasive species to the United States, mostly to Florida. Everglades Park officials suggested that thousands may live within the park, and that the species has been breeding there for some years. More recent data suggest that these pythons would not withstand winter climates north of Florida, but contradicting previous research shows that they have been traveling significantly beyond the tropical climates of the southeast.

The python is among the longest snake species and extant retiles in the world. Many stories have surfaced about twenty-foot pythons loose in the Ozarks and Missouri, and another eighteen-footer was found in a pantry in Orange County. Although they don't usually breed in the wild, in most states many people keep them as exotic pets, including a biology teacher at our school. Evidently, they survive fine in the winter in a terrarium with a heat lamp.

This python was a sweet and cuddly thing named Monty. His owner was a biology teacher you have already heard of, Dr. J, the tarantula capturer of chapter 10. He was eight feet long and weighed fifty-four pounds—the snake, not the teacher. Whenever the custodians found or caught a mouse, it would go right into the python's aquarium straight away, where the snake would coil itself around the rodent and squeeze it, then swallow it whole. Most of the kids—the boys, at least—loved the big snake. They liked to watch it eat, and they liked to hold it, and of course, they loved to tease the girls with the massive reptile.

But Monty the Python's heart belong to Dr. J. Whenever the students would hold him, Monty would wrap around their shoulders, then gravitate toward Dr. J. Wherever he was in the room, the snake's tongue would protrude to locate him, and his head would move away from the student, and his body would stretch out toward the teacher. It was a fascinating, if not creepy, phenomenon.

It was reported to the main office that the top of the aquarium where Monty lived had been left off and forgotten for several class periods of the day. When the teacher finally checked on the animal at the end of the day before he left, the snake was gone. Disappeared. He had stealthily made his way out of the enclosure, out of the room, down some obscure hallway, and was now somewhere else other than the classroom.

Because pythons only eat large live animals and only four to five times a year, there was no real worry about killings, deaths, and destruction. But its presence, unattended in the school, made for some very uneasy female students and staff members in the various offices around the school. The main worry that the biology teachers had was for the safety of the rodents, rabbits, and hamsters still housed in the biology classrooms.

As in the case of Beverly, the wayward tarantula, Monty the python jokes began almost immediately. Monty the python has escaped; he is looking for the *Meaning of Life*. Monty the python, something *Completely Different*. Monty, the snake who says Ni, trying to find his *Holy Grail*. Maybe taking a line from that movie, Monty was just trying to "run away! Run away!"

The story of the missing snake spread like autumn leaves off a maple tree in a wind storm. Kids trying to dissuade their parents from attending the conferences with the teachers painted a picture of huge snakes dangling on the filing cabinets and/or slithering through the lobby. This would have been great billing for our Halloween fundraiser:

Haunted Hallways with real snakes and spiders!

However, it was not so great for the promotion of our goal to have every parent attend the parent-teacher conferences. We weren't sure, but we think that some of the kids had the idea that their parents, especially their moms, would avoid PTCs with the news that a large snake was roaming free and unconfined in the building.

It worked! Mothers called the office days before the event, wanting to know about the snake.

"Is it true?" they would ask. "Is there really an escaped snake?"

They wanted to know how big it was. Had it been seen or apprehended yet? Are the students in any danger? My person favorite statement was "I am not coming to the school if a boa constrictor may fall out of the ceiling into my lap!"

We had parents calling to say they would not come to school to meet with anybody about anything until the snake was found. Perfectly rational human beings were scared out of their wits, and panic ensued like a bad horror movie. Children told stories of animals disappearing and weird noises in the pipes. Our librarian, Mr. Calder, would unlock the library doors in the morning, creep in quietly, and call out, "Here, Monty, Monty, Monty. Come out, come out wherever you are."

Monty didn't come out. In fact, he didn't show his round face and pudgy body for several days. Nevertheless, the whole building—nay, the entire community—was on edge.

Two days before parent-teacher conferences were to take place, Mrs. Bell's English class was reading *The Adventures of Tom Sawyer* and having a lively discussion about the character flaws of Injun Joe when suddenly a blood curdling scream rang out. It traveled through the third floor hallway, down the stairwell and into her classroom. Needless to say, the students were not only startled but a bit unnerved by the loud cry that seemed to be coming through door and the vents directly to the room. They looked to Mrs. Bell, who, with a knowing smile and a raised eyebrow, said,

"Well, I guess someone finally found the missing snake."

Her words were corroborated a few minutes later when the principal's voice came over the intercom confirming that the wayward snake had indeed been located. However, it had not yet been captured, but they were "pretty sure" where he was hiding.

As it turned out, the stories were not far off. After eight days on the lamb, a trace of Monty was found in the form of a skin that had been shed outside of a heat duct vent in a third-floor classroom. A district maintenance man was doing some duct work and found a snakeskin-like material on the floor outside a heating vent. Pythons like to live in warm, dry climates, like Africa, where pythons are plentiful, so this should have been a clue for us when Monty first went missing.

One of the biology teachers confirmed that it was, indeed, Monty's skin and concluded that he must have shed it before venturing into the duct. No kidding. The only questions remaining were (1) "Was the python still in there?" and (2) "How were we to recover him?" A crew of six men assembled to consider the possibilities—capture by committee, if you will—when a woman, outside the group offered,

"Let's leave something for it to eat just outside the vent and wait for him to come and get it."

They were considering crafting just the right tool to reach in and grab the snake or fashioning a stick with a mirror and a flashlight on the end to observe it. After much hemming and hawing, the guys agreed that the come-and-get-it lunch was the best course of action. They removed the vent cover, then left a half of ham sandwich outside the opening.

Now, larger pythons, the twenty-five-foot kind, eat larger animals from rabbits to small deer. Smaller snakes, like our Monty, eat much smaller prey like cats, mice, rats, and other rodents. However, the larger the meal, the longer between meal times the snake can go without eating. Some snakes might only eat four or five times per year while others might eat four to five times per week. Since we didn't have a whole lot of rabbits and cats in our vents, our snake might be hungry right away. Or depending on how many mice he's found in the building, he might not need to eat for a while. A trap was set, and we all hoped that Monty would be ready for a snake snack sooner rather than later.

It was only a few hours later when Monty made his big entrance sliding out of the vent in a wavy serpentine motion to grab the sandwich, and he landed right in a rather large net that had been laid to nab him. Unfortunately, a female student was in the room when the large python appeared. Thus, the blood-curdling scream.

The maintenance men were again called, and it took two of them to wrap the snake and carry it back to his terrarium, sweet terrarium. Relief fell over the school like silence on a daycare at naptime.

If we'd had munchkins, they would have belted out a chorus of "*Ding-dong*, the snake is dead!" However, we didn't have munchkins, and the snake was very much alive. Totally and finally, Monty the python was recovered unharmed and returned to his home where he lived comfortably and happily ever after.

Parent-teacher conferences were well-attended by parents and students and went off without a hitch. Both the python and the students were unscathed, except possibly those who were failing math.

CHAPTER 12

EVERYONE AND THEIR DOGS

All of us occasionally have those days at work when it seems like everyone and their dog has to come in for one thing or another, interrupting a quiet, efficient working environment that is the main office, the beating heart of the school. This noteworthy morning, it literally happened in our not-so-quiet, not-entirely-efficient main office.

We were all scurrying around, doing secretary things, giving the beating heart of our school a serious workout, when a little old lady came rushing in, carrying her dog, a copper-colored dachshund that looked like it hadn't missed a single meal in many years. This little lady was walking very determinedly with a purpose, and she nearly knocked two football players over as she hastened through the door.

"'Cuse me, ma'am," one of them said in a deep voice as she sideswiped him. The group looked at the little German woman and her dog and snickered as she left them in her wake.

"My name is Mrs. Van Heffner. I live in the neighborhood, and I need to talk to someone in charge about my dog," she blurted out, not really waiting her turn as there were several others in line at the counter ahead of her. Conversation at the counter ceased for several seconds, except for the mailman who was desperately trying to get someone's signature for a package.

"Excuse me, can *you* help me?" he pleaded with Cami, one of the secretaries, as he gave Mrs. Van Hefner a sideways glance that said, "Wait your turn, Grandma." Then it began again with everyone talking at once.

"I need a street pass to go home," one student whined.

"Can I get a ream of paper for the library?" another student interjected.

"How can I find out where the bus is going to take me after school?" came the small voice of a timid, new ninth grader.

It was a lovely mid-May morning, and spring was inching closer and closer, which meant for us that spring break and the end of the school year was very close at hand. This was the time of year, as the end crept nearer, that the teachers became a little shorter on patience and the office staff had a tough time keeping both students and parents happy and on track heading into yearbooks and graduation. Mrs. Van Heffner was a short woman, seventy-five to eighty years old, sporting a heavy wool coat. She was also wearing the brightest shade of orange lipstick I'd ever seen, and her hair was a shocking bright rust color. Her cheeks had a bit too much rouge, and her eyebrows were drawn on thick and unevenly. Clearly, she'd spent a bit of time getting ready to take her dog for his morning walk. Being a dog lover, I stepped over to her, leaving the rest of the chaos at the other end of the counter wondering what her definition of "in charge" was, and said,

"How may I help the two of you?" I reached out to pet the animal.

She seemed oblivious of the group of people needing assistance, and she looked at me as though she might cry. Her bottom lip began to quiver, and she said,

"I need to talk to someone in your archery department. One of their arrows just hit my dog as we were walking through the park." She held up the arrow as evidence of her story, and I jumped back a bit to ensure it would not hit me.

She was stroking the dog's fur and cooing in his ear. While he was enjoying the attention, he was clearly annoyed with her breath tickling his ear, and he was squirming to get free of her grip. He didn't look as if he was in any discomfort, aside from her fussing over him, and he sure didn't look as though he'd just been shot by an arrow. He wasn't howling, yipping, or bleeding; however, I could see *she* was very distressed, and so I treated her with as much compassion as I could muster on a crazy busy morning in the main office. A few of the group began looking in our direction, so I led her to a chair, where she could sit with the weight of the dog in her arms.

"What a fat little dog!" came a comment from someone at the counter. This did not please Mrs. Van Hefner one bit.

"He's mommy's big boy!" She snorted and kissed the dog, then she turned her attention to me, ignoring the snip who had insulted her dog and her indirectly.

"Tell me what happened," I encouraged her to tell me the whole story.

"Fritz and I were walking around the park." I noted to myself that he could use a bit of exercise but said nothing as she continued. "We came around the corner to the path that runs next to the track behind the school when this arrow came flying out of nowhere and hit him." This time, she thrust the arrow in my direction, and I lifted my arm in reflex. I reached out to take it from her so she wouldn't hurt me or anyone else.

Her voice began rising, and I could see she was getting herself all worked up again. She was drawing the attention of the staff as well as the patrons at the counter, a few of whom were getting very annoyed with the situation.

"Hey, I was here first," one impatient father who had indeed been waiting for a few minutes interrupted her story.

"Let me try to calm her down," I implored, "then I will be right with you."

With a heavy sigh, he went back to the counter to try to illicit someone else's help.

"Can *you* please help me?" the mailman asked again of no one in particular. He received no response and instead sat in the chair next to Mrs. Van Hefner and also began petting the animal.

I was mesmerized by her cantaloupe lips and noticed that the color had been applied just outside the line of her lips. The mailman was also watching her lips as she spoke. I wondered what his subconscious reaction was to them. I consciously pulled my attention back to her story. I put my hand on her arm and patted it as I asked,

"Your dog's name is Fritz?" I was thinking Tank might have been a more apt name for the overweight beast.

"Yes!" she wailed with fresh tears rolling down her cheeks. "And now he's been shot with an arrow. Oh, my poor baby!"

Collectively, everyone at the counter turned around to look at the woman and the dog to see if he was mortally wounded. Seeing nothing of note, they went back to trying to accomplish their business.

She explained to me and the mailman how she had sent him through rattlesnake training, although it had not been proven if it was effective yet. Clearly, the dog had not been through any such bow-and-arrow training. If he had, that certainly hadn't been money well spent.

She cried some more and buried her face in her dog's coat, leaving carrot-colored lip prints on his fur. Fritz gave me a see-what-I-have-to-live-with look over her shoulder, and I am quite sure if he could have rolled his eyes he would have at that moment. But you could tell that he was loving the attention and the spotlight, believing that he was the star of the moment, which he was, I guess. I gave her a minute to compose herself and hoped that everyone in the office wasn't staring at us. I looked up to see our little drama had been lost on everyone there.

At this moment, the dachshund wriggled free of her grip and jumped down off her lap. I took a quick inventory of his pudgy body to see if there was a bull's-eye on him anywhere. Not finding one, I retrieved him and returned him to his mistress's arms. I lifted with my legs so as not to hurt my back under his girth, then I turned my attention back to Ms. Van Hefner.

Seeing how distressed she was, I tried to keep from cracking a smile at her dramatics and began explaining that we did not, if fact, have an archery department or program or even an archery class. At this news, she began to cry even harder.

"Heavens to Betsy. You don't care about little Fritz," she bemoaned. "This is just dreadful!"

At this declaration, the mailman actually laughed out loud, and she gave him a look that shot its own little arrows. He picked this time to leave his chair next to her in search of his much-needed signature. I thought to myself that "little" wouldn't quite be the word I would use to describe Fritz.

"Of course, I do," I assured her as I again took in the size and weight of the dog. I reached over to pet him again, more to reassure him than to appease her.

"Do you walk Fritz every day?" I asked.

"Every day," she echoed as she nodded.

"Has there ever been trouble with arrows before?" She shook her head. "You know, we don't really teach archery here," I said delicately, hoping she would take the news well.

She turned her face completely away from me. She wasn't much interested in my explanation or what I had to say, and I wondered how I was going to convince her that we hadn't trained archers in the school district since the medieval times. I tried to think if the Boy Scouts of America troop in our neighborhood still offered an archery merit badge anymore. My mind was wandering again instead of listening intently to her story.

Archery has been around for literally 64,001 years. Originating in Africa, it spread to Australia, Europe, and the Americas. The medieval times, during the fourteenth and fifteenth centuries, were archery's Golden Era. Not only was everyone expected to have a bow and arrows, but they were expected to be proficient in using them. Real emphasis was put on training soldiers with longbows and arrows during the 100 Years War, and I found myself wondering if this little grandma and her dog had been around for that.

Archers were held in great admiration then; I am sure they didn't run around shooting their arrows at innocent overweight dogs. They trained with great care and learned their craft with great precision. They wore highly decorated bracers (arm guards) and used fine leather grips and often were trained to shoot barefoot to ensure stability and improve accuracy. I am quite sure that none of this applied to our archery classes—I mean, if we had archery classes. Once more,

I pulled myself back to the moment and listened to her description of the events of the morning.

When she was done, several facts occurred to me: First and foremost, she was a totally devoted dog owner. I was convinced that she was probably more devoted to Fritz than to Mr. Van Heffner. I have seen some spoiled dogs and may have even owned a few, but this dog looked as if he would be totally content with a paw massage with aromatherapy oil and a nap in a spa robe when he was done with his walk.

Secondly, if in fact she was walking parallel to the track, that would mean that there was a football field, two sets of bleachers, a softball diamond, plus the track between Fritz and any place that our archers might be attempting to shoot any arrows. Next, if we were training archers for the next 100 Years War, they probably would not be able to hit a small-ish twenty-pound dachshund that stood only ten inches from the ground over the trees lining the park as he was trotting. I sincerely doubt that their accuracy would be *that* good.

Last of all, *if* we did have an archery class and *if* they had been practicing and *if* their arrows had made it that distance through the trees and located that one short dog, it would be highly unlikely that the arrow would have enough velocity to hit the animal, and *if* it did, it would probably just bounce off his round portly body. I came to the conclusion that it probably was one or more of our students who might be playing a prank on Mrs. Van Heffner. It was more likely that they threw the arrow like a dart from some nearby bushes rather than shooting it with a bow.

But I knew that Mrs. Van Heffner would not be satisfied with that enlightenment, so I listened closely for the most part to her story, and I commiserated with her dog who seemed to be just as possessive of her as she was of him. I offered her a Styrofoam cup of water, and I assured her that I would indeed have a discussion with the archery teacher and let him know in no uncertain terms that he and his archers must be more vigilant where they were aiming their arrows and what they were using for targets.

"Tell them they must be careful. We walk there every morning," she reiterated.

"I will tell them that there are many dog owners that walk there with their pets, and I will let them know that there will be consequences if anything like this should happen again," I stressed, hoping she wouldn't ask what those consequences would be.

I must admit that I was trying to come up with the name of a teacher that I didn't much like to send her in search of, maybe that mean English teacher on the third floor who was so tough on the kids. This grandma would be a good match for her; but instead, I told her that I would take care of her problem as quickly as I possibly could. I went out on a limb and guaranteed that nothing like this would ever happen again, and I said all of it with all the sincerity that she was hoping for *and* with a straight face. She gave me a long steady stare, her lopsided eyebrows furrowing over her nose, and I couldn't tell if she was assessing my sincerity or putting a curse on me.

In the end, she seemed to accept that I would do what I promised. She set little Fritz on the floor. Half dragging him by his leash, she made her way out of the office toward the front doors of the building. As soon as he was in the hallway, he began yapping at passersby, and as soon as they reached the outer doors to the building, he was barking wildly at everyone and their dogs passing our school on their way to the park.

I watched her and Fritz walk out of the parking lot.

"Watch out for errant flying arrows," I silently warned them, as we never did discover where the lone arrow came from or if there might be more coming.

As a postscript, I did pass along the information that Mrs. Van Heffner gave me to the gym teacher, who was the closest teacher I could find to archery. I gave him the arrow as I relayed the story of the woman and her dog. He laughed and laughed and noted,

"It probably wouldn't be the best idea for us to arm our students with bows and arrows."

It was my turn to laugh now as I had been holding it in so as not to upset Mrs. Van Hefner.

"Agreed," I said as I turned to go back to the office to find out what the rest of the day had to offer.

CHAPTER 13

LIFE IS BETTER WITH A SMART DOG

And speaking of dogs . . . this chapter has nothing to do with school, students, bus drivers, and such, but I have a few things I would like to say about our dogs. Both my husband and I love dogs and have owned them all our lives. They enrich our existence, and our lives just wouldn't be as full without them.

When we were first married, he had a six-year old seventy-five-pound golden Labrador named Mister. He was the color of a perfectly toasted marshmallow, and he had the IQ and temperament of a toasted marshmallow too. He was strong and athletic and dumb as a stump, but a cream puff on the inside, unless something or someone went after his family or his dog. His dog was my sixteen-pound Jack Russell terrier who was a year older whose name was BB.

There was a comic named Patrice O'Neal who once quipped about Labs having the best PR of all the dogs, because they really are daft, but still billed as one of the smartest, most popular dog breeds in our country.

Recently, we lost our Lab, Mister, due to a large tumor in his abdomen. He was thirteen years old, but he was a puppy right up to the time he passed. He was most definitely toy motivated, especially if it was any kind of a ball. He was crazy for tennis balls and would chase a tennis ball as long as you would throw it. He would swim halfway across a lake just to get his waterlogged tennis ball and bring it back for you to throw again.

We had a pool table in our basement, and he would like to stand up at the rail and just watch those colored balls roll around the green felt and disappear into the pockets. He would listen as they would go down through the table and finally settle in the ball return at the end. He would run to the end of the table and see them there, and then he'd come back to go through the entire exercise again.

Our home was built so that you could walk out of the back door on the main level right onto a deck that overlooked the backyard. In the basement, there was another sliding glass door that led outside to the grass level of the yard. Mister loved his yard and loved to be outside, so we had dog doors in every door so he could go outside whenever he wanted. He would collect all his toys and take them out so he could have them near him and play any time the urge struck him.

My husband, Jeff, had some extra time on his hands one afternoon while he and Mister were home alone. He e decided that would be the perfect opportunity to practice his pool game. Mister had other ideas. After doing a few honey-dos, he headed downstairs and spent an hour or so running racks and practicing some drills. After a while, he went to the kitchen to grab a sandwich. He was there for a short time and was surprised that the dog had not followed him to his favorite room to see what was there to snack on, but the lively Lab didn't come up. He went back downstairs to finish up his drills and strolled to the end of the table to retrieve the balls from the ball return. To his surprise, there were no balls on the table, but even more astonishing was that there were only a couple of balls in the ball return rather than the fifteen balls he had expected.

He thought maybe there was some obstacle preventing the balls from following the track inside the table to the ball return, and he was contemplating how to proceed to find the problem. As he stood considering what to do next, Mister came in through the dog door, casting a sideways glance at his owner. He walked all the way around the table—actually, he skulked to the end where the balls collected. Once there, he put his big head into the ball return, pulled it back out, and headed toward the door.

"Mister?" Jeff beckoned the dog.

He stopped and considered not waiting to see why his master was calling, but when he turned and looked up, Jeff could see the bright orange paint of the five-ball showing under his jowls as he gently carried the ball. He calculated and decided to stop and immediately dropped the ball where he stood. The ball rolled away from the large dog to Jeff's feet where he bent over and picked up the slimy pool ball.

Mister put his head down and slowly made his way to the stairs to escape. Jeff called the Lab, who reluctantly returned to his side, and they both walked over the sliding glass door. Once there, he could see all the brightly colored balls in a pile on the lawn in the backyard.

He looked down at the dog, and Mister returned his gaze, wagging his tail as if to say, "See what I did?"

And to the unasked question, my husband replied aloud, "Yes, I see what you did."

The tail wagged even faster.

My kids and husband liked to make up voices that our dogs would have it they could actually talk. Usually these were goofy cartoon voices making the animal seem nonsensical and daftly charming. I agree with Orhan Pamuk, who wrote, "Dogs do speak, but only to those who listen."

The pool balls were not the only thing that Mister took outside; there were many objects that ended up in the yard. Most every toy that Mister ever had ended up in the yard many times all through the winter, only to be found when the snow melted in the spring, as many dog owners will tell you.

My youngest son, Q, came home from school one day just as Mister was coming out of the dog door with a box of crackers in his mouth. He stopped and looked at the boy, then turned with the box still in his mouth and headed right back inside. Once inside, he turned to see the door open and my son step inside. He immediately dropped the box, lay down, and gave his cutest "am I in trouble?" look.

But the best dog door story was the year Mister was a good dog and received a giant rawhide bone from Santa. Mister loved rawhides almost as much as tennis balls, and my husband made sure that every night he was given a fresh new bone to chew on so that we could sleep at night without the dog waking us up wanting to play or go for a walk. It got to the point that if there was a bone lying around with teeth marks on it, Mister would spit it out and sit and stare at him until he was given a new one.

However, the big one he got for Christmas lasted quite a while, and even though it had a few teeth marks, he carried that bone around everywhere. The day came when he wanted to take the giant bone outside. My husband and I were sitting on the couch, watching some TV when our beloved Lab came into the room with his beloved bone and headed toward the beloved dog door. Needless to say, that bone was not going to go out of that door the way he had it in him mouth, and we watched curiously to see what he was going to do.

He tried to walk right through the small flap with the bone protruding out each side of his jowls. He was stopped cold. The next time he backed up a bit and got a bit of a running start. He was going at a pretty good clip the next time he hit the door and kind of bounced off it with a perplexed look, clearly not understanding the botheration.

He tried just standing in front of the door, just trying to force the bone through instead of running at it. After several minutes of this tactic, my husband and I were busting up, and I was just about to go to him and help him out, but Jeff put his hand on mine and said, "No. Let's just wait and see if he can figure it out."

The dog dropped the bone at the door and lay down facing the flap with his front paws folded in front of his chest. He lay there several minutes looking from the bone to the flap as his brain turned and churned. He didn't move much, didn't cock his head or whimper at all. He just stared at the bone, then at the door, trying to wrap his mind around the problem.

Finally, he made it work in his head. He stood up, stepped over the bone, and walked out of the dog door, leaving the giant rawhide on the rug. We watched in amazement as he then stuck his head back through the door, grabbed one end of the bone, and dragged it outside. My husband was so proud that his big dumb Lab figured it out all on his own and conquered the bone.

This was the dog that believed that if he was under the covers and you couldn't see him, you would not know he was there. He would sit with a sheet or blanket over his head and truly believe that he was invisible. You could walk through the room, and he would hear you and sit up and turn his head toward your movement, but he would think that because you had not made eye contact you didn't know he was watching you from beneath.

He would continually break in to Q's room to find trouble of one sort or another. His shoes and socks would end up all over the house, and food wrappers from the garbage would mysteriously end up in the yard. No matter what he tried, Q could not keep the dog outside his door. We would be fixing dinner or watching a movie, and we'd hear Q say,

"Get out of my room, Mister!" Just like an older brother scolding a younger one for getting into his stuff.

For his next trick, Mister will conquer a chicken. That's right, a whole chicken. We were expecting our kids for dinner one night, which was already prepared and waiting to be devoured by our two boys. We were downstairs, Jeff watching TV and I was banging balls around on the pool table.

"Have you seen the dog?" I inquired as he was usually wherever we were in the house.

"Nope." He replied, unfazed that his pride and joy was not right at his side.

Precisely at that moment, Mister crept literally into the room. My husband watched him and asked, "Did you scold the dog over something?"

"Nope," I replied, unmoved that the dog might have had his feelings hurt.

When I looked over, the large honey colored dog was sitting in the corner of the room, with his nose facing the paneling, his head hanging low.

"What in the world is wrong with him?" I wondered out loud.

My husband was worried he might be sick while I suspected more of an I've-done-something-bad vibe going on. I looked around to see if anything was broken or missing, then I walked upstairs to the kitchen. Everything seemed normal. I turned on the lights and surveyed the room. On the surface, everything seemed as it should be.

Our little Jack Russell terrier, BB, followed me into the kitchen and began sniffing around, then she began licking the floor intensely. I looked on the counter for the rotisserie chicken that had been purchased earlier that evening and did not see it. I looked in the fridge, wondering what my husband had done with it. It was not there either. I walked back downstairs to find him trying to console the distraught Labrador.

"Did you do something with the chicken that was for dinner?" I asked.

"No. It was on the counter the last time I saw it," he said distractedly.

Then it hit us both at the same time. We ran upstairs where the terrier was now licking the side of the range, and we began searching for the chicken. We never found it; all that was left was the disposable container that had been discarded in the backyard. Our precious dog had jumped up on the counter, dragged the container with the chicken off the edge, spilling juice down the side of the cupboard and the oven, and he devoured the entire thing. Meat, bones, juice, and part of the packaging were all gone. To hide his crime, he had taken the rest of the package outside presumably to conceal the evidence of his misconduct.

Needless to say, I was furious, and so was my terrier, BB, because all she had gotten from the feast was the juice that was left behind. My husband, however, was now *worried* about his dog.

"He will never be able to digest all those bones." He fussed and fretted and immediately got on the telephone to the veterinarian. The vet assured him that Mister would survive the event as long as your wife doesn't kill him but told us we should feed him oatmeal for forty-eight hours to help the bones pass smoothly through his digestive system.

"That's great!" I exclaimed with thick sarcasm. "So his punishment for eating the whole chicken is that he now *has* to eat oatmeal and milk for two days. Probably ought to put a little brown sugar and some raisins in it too," I added disdainfully.

It was a win-win for the dog; he did in fact survive. He survived both the chicken and my wrath, and he lived to have many other adventures, much to my chagrin.

The one thing Mister loved more than tennis balls or chicken or Jeff was the water. That dog was born to swim. When he was just a few months old, we took him to Jeff's cousin's house for a BBQ. They had just put in a new swimming pool in their backyard, and before we could even say hello and put our things down, we heard a splash, and Mister was swimming in the new pool with their Lab, Smoky Joe.

If we were driving to the lake for a swim, he could sense when we were getting nearer to water. He would be in the back of the truck, and he would open the door of the shell with his nose and start barking and going crazy at just the sight of a lake. The lakes in and around our mountains were quite far away, but it was always a relaxing drive and a fun day to take the dogs for a picnic and a swim on a summer weekend. Mister would bark and yap and let everyone in the neighborhoods and the canyons know that he was out for a drive! We would pull into a parking place after arriving then turn him loose, and before we could even get our stuff out of the truck, we would hear in the distance a huge splash as Mister dived into the water.

We would set up chairs on the beach, and Jeff and Mister would play in the water. Jeff would throw a tennis ball as far as he could from the beach, and Mister would swim effortlessly to it and retrieve it for hours or until we had to stop because he was so tired, but he would never stop himself. One of the last trips we ever took with him to the lake, he was quite a bit older but still had the heart and desire to both climb and swim.

It was busy, and we had to park a bit farther than we normally did, but Mister was raring to go. Our usual spot was already taken, and we had to park at the top of a bluff and hike down. The other side was a steep embankment, and I wasn't sure our old dog would be able to climb back up after our afternoon was over because of his age.

Mister barreled over the side; Jeff tried to stop him, worried that if he had to go down after his dog, neither one of them would make it back. We peered over the side of the cliff; we looked and could not see him. We called and called as we walked along the edge. Even the little terrier was looking and yapping for the Lab. All three of us were standing shoulder to shoulder, fretting and worrying and peering over the edge, and Jeff was just about to go down the face of the sea cliff when I looked to my left and saw Mister standing right there beside me, looking over the edge, wagging his tail. He looked up at me beaming happily as if to say, "Hey, what are we all looking at?"

Not only had he found a way up somewhere down the beach but had climbed the steep grade and found us calling for him. We laughed about it all the way home, and as I think back on all the crazy things he did and how he made our lives so much richer and happier, I couldn't help but think that life was better with a dog, and I wondered how life would be with a smart dog.

I would not find out the answer to that riddle with our next set of dogs, Jazzie and Jeter. Jazzie was a whippet mix. She was a little fourteen-pound bundle of what-are-we-going-to-do-next? Definitely more energy than brains. She was lithe and athletic, all legs with a cute little face covered in freckles and two black eyes. She always looked like she had just been in a fight.

I was quietly sitting on my patio one hot summer night, listening to the crickets and enjoying a glass of wine, while Jazz was curiously checking the perimeter of the yard, which she did daily and nightly and probably a couple of times throughout the afternoon while I was at work. She would sort of hop on three legs because she didn't like the feel of the grass on her feet. Frequently, she would pee while standing on her two front legs so her back feet wouldn't touch the ground. When she made her nightly patrol, she would use the stepping stones placed around the yard.

This evening, Jazzie was creeping about, stretching her long legs and her feet barely touching the ground, when all of a sudden, she jumped in the air, all four feet leaving the ground at once. It was like she'd been shocked with a shocker collar or some mysterious jolt. I thought for a minute she'd been stung by a bee, but her tail was wagging furiously. She didn't yip or yelp, so I knew she was okay, and she had a big smile on her face, so I knew she was enjoying herself.

Then she did it again, and that's when I saw it. A grasshopper. It jumped up, just in front of her face, high above her head, and landed in the grass before her. Then she jumped, exactly the same way after it. I was like she was trying to mimic the insect's motion. It would jump, and she would jump to pounce on it and miss it because it would jump again, then she would jump again. This ritual went on for several minutes as she chased the bug around our backyard. Springing up on her athletic back legs, trying to catch her prey. She would come so close, and it would barely escape her clutches.

Then she got it! She caught it in her mouth and immediately spit it out, I'm sure, because it was wiggling and kicking her tongue. I suspected that if she was able, she would be laughing and giggling up a storm. The funniest thing was when she spit it out and it stopped jumping, she couldn't figure out why.

She kept pushing it with her nose trying to get the insect to resume their wonderful game. The bug had one last jump in his legs, and he made it to where the fence met the grass, and that is where he crawled under and made his escape. Jazzie watched the place he disappeared for a few minutes, sniffing and looking for her new friend, then she was off and on to the next escapade. Life was always an adventure for her as it should be for all of us!

My Chihuahua-terrier mix, Jeter, was a totally different animal. No, really, he was a different animal. He was roommates with Jazzie, as Mister had been with BB a few years earlier. He was a short little fat thing with squatty legs and a body like a hefty brick. He had one Chihuahua ear which stood straight up on the left side of his small head; on the other side was a bent terrier ear which flopped when he trotted. He was not at all adventurous or daring and was deathly afraid of thunder. He had shirts to help him and a sound-proof indoor doghouse, but those only helped minimally. The only thing he required that he didn't have was his own therapist, and that dog needed *serious* therapy.

He didn't have a brave bone in his stocky tank-like body. He was a six-year-old train wreck but cute as a ladybug on a leaf. He liked to go to the park on his own terms, of course, and once in a great while, he would chase his counterpart, Jazzie, and try for about fifteen seconds to catch her, but she would sprint away like a missile, and he considered it too much energy expenditure to chase after her.

No, Jeter was a dog of leisure; he was a rescue dog that came to us from an abusive home, and he took to the good life well. His favorite activity was taking a nap. He was the sleepingest dog you ever saw. He would snooze any time or place. His favorite way to get some exercise was to lie by the treadmill as I walked and try to figure out how it worked. You could just see his little brain working to solve the mystery of the contraption until it was too much for him, then he'd sprawl on his side and fall asleep. Apparently, watching someone else walk on the treadmill is exhausting!

Smart they weren't, but they were joyful, funny, and more wonderful companions could not be found anywhere. They were adored and spoiled by us, and we were loved and cherished by them, our dogs, our friends.

PART FOUR

ARE YOU GOING TO EAT THAT?

CHAPTER 14

ALL THE GUM AND NOTHING BUT THE GUM

I tried to teach my kids from an early age to think for themselves. I thought this was prudent and a good idea at the time. Then came the day when my offspring actually began to think for themselves. Then I asked myself,

"What the Thomas Aquinas were you thinking?"

From the eighth grade to graduation from high school, my oldest son thought that he had thinking for himself nailed down. At that time, as most teenagers, he had less interest in being a student and doing what mom wanted and more interest in girls, peers, and all the things that mom just doesn't understand. I guess he was not so different than your children at that age.

When he turned sixteen, he suddenly had an irresistible urge to have a squid tattoo inked on his arm. For months, I told him no, and I argued my reasons beautifully. I explained to him the consequences of meaningless permanent body art (maybe not the best way to start), the risks of infections, etc. It's expensive, painful, and hard to get rid of, I argued. Sure, it looks cool now, but what about in ten, twenty, or thirty years.

The debate about tats between teenagers and parents has been a long and arduous one. However, after all my efforts to dissuade him from his colorful pursuit, one day he came to me with an entire presentation on why he should be able to get a tattoo. It was very well prepared, bullet points, research, pictures, the whole nine yards. He had statistics, numbers, cost comparisons, and analysis; the only thing he was missing was a pointer, a suit and tie. All I could think was "If only he would put forth this kind of effort in his schoolwork, we'd never have arguments about turning in homework or you-are-never-going-to-graduate-with-that-GPA discussions."

In the end, I told him he had to wait until he was eighteen and was a little more mature to make lifelong decisions. For his eighteenth birthday, his girlfriend bought him his beloved tattoo, which he still has to this day, his first of a few colorful creations that adorn his body. He married the girl and still has her too.

The reason I bring this up is that I recently read a paper written by a seventh grader in the Midwest about students being allowed to chew gum in school. It was well written and outlined with several details which were directly on point. Her thesis was, not only should gum be allowed in class, but the teachers should supply it to help relieve stress in students, help them focus, and make them relax so they are more open to learning and studying.

Her arguments were nicely written, and like my son's tattoo presentation, she also had research, analysis, statistics, and relevant documented facts. She argued that if gum were allowed, her fellow schoolmates might throw it away rather than being sneaky and sticking it under the desk. Some students may put it under the desk or on the floor just to be rebellious, but if they had the privilege of chewing gum at school, they might be more respectful. If it is too loud, as some teachers say it is, all the teacher needs to do is to ask them not to blow bubbles, problem solved.

"More than a privilege, it should be a right," she claimed.

I know that if you are a teacher, you are probably at least giving me a chuckle right about now, but if you are a seventh or eighth grader, you are probably cheering her on.

"You go, girl!"

I found myself wondering if this was actually an assignment that she had done for her social studies class, and I wondered if she put this much work into all her assignments. Like the struggle between parents and teens regarding tattoos, the struggle between teachers and students concerning gum chewing in class is a timeless one that will probably continue through the ages in education.

From the first day of kindergarten, 99 percent of teachers are going to tell their students, "Don't chew gum in class."

Their reasons: it's rude, it's noisy, it's distracting, and it's messy. They might also say, "Don't chew gun in unless you have enough for everyone."

However, I always thought this a lame argument because if it's messy, noisy, and distracting why would you want all twenty-five kids in your class chewing gum at the same time?

I've known teachers that will stand at the door with their hand out and make all the kids that are chewing gum when they enter the room to spit it in their hand. EEEWWW! Gross. Others I've seen have a wooden dowel that they make the kids stick their gum to, which is even worse because then everybody has to stare at it all day. Of course, if the kids are smart, they'll hold it in their cheek until they are in class, but only if they are smart enough to think of this in time.

Some school districts prohibit the habit all together, others leave it up to the discretion of the teacher. Most teachers do not want the distraction of gum or any snack in their classroom, and most principals do not want the sticky, messy, gooey stuff in their buildings, and most custodians would agree.

Cleaning up gum was always a challenge for the custodians in our school. Almost immediately after the end of the school year in June, the process of cleaning the entire school begins. From the bathroom floors to the drinking fountains, everything needs to be cleaned. One of the biggest projects was removing the gum from every place in the school that students had found to stick it, and students were very good at finding new and creative places to stick the gum that they technically weren't allowed to chew. So a big chunk of summertime was spent on the not-so-enviable task of scraping gum.

Bud, our one hundred-year-old custodian who was doing everything he could to avoid retirement and not have to stay at home every day with his wife, was in charge of eradicating the gum from the auditorium floor. He was slow in both mind and body, he moved at the speed of drying paint, and his thoughts turned sluggishly when they turned. Bud had worked for the school district as a custodian for nearly forty years. He had a full head of hair atop his scalp, and he had another full head of hair which covered his chin, concealed his upper lip, invaded his nostrils, protruded from his ears, and shaded his eyes like a visor.

We had many pics of Bud taking five or ten or twenty minutes sleeping in whatever chair he happened to be passing and landed in during his shift. One of these pics actually showed Bud dozing in a chair with his feet on a desk while the garbage can next to it was overflowing with trash. Our head custodian, Dick, would wake Bud, and he would jump with a start, stretch his long arthritic limbs, and reluctantly rise ever so slowly to tackle his next task.

One of these mornings, the task was to scrape the gum, all of the gum, from the auditorium floor. A simple task, one might say. Tedious, perhaps, but straightforward and very important if we didn't want the gum to pile up into disgusting speed bumps in the aisles and between the seats.

Bud began the job after his second break of the morning with his trusty scraper in hand. He began diligently working his way across each row. Each time Dick, the head custodian, checked on him, Bud seemed to be focused on the mission and was making good progress from the front of the large auditorium to the back rows.

When he was done, which was surprisingly speedy, he settled back into his chair in the office, complaining that he was late in taking his lunch break and that his back was beginning to hurt from an old football injury. Dick agreed that Bud had done well to finish the auditorium floor quicker than expected and decided that lunch should be the next order of business.

After they ate, Dick headed to the auditorium to survey the work Bud had spent the morning accomplishing. Bud moved in the opposite direction like and old hound dog looking forward to an afternoon nap. In the auditorium, imagine Dick's surprise when he walked up the aisles, looking between the rows and finding gum, all the gum, still there, *everywhere*! Incredulous and trying desperately to keep his composure, he confronted Bud, who was lazily pushing a broom through the commons area.

"I thought you told me that you scraped all the gum in the auditorium." Dick's voice shook as he spoke. "What were you doing in there all morning?" The volume was rising.

Bud's face registered disbelief.

"I did." Bud looked at him with eyes wide. "I scraped up every piece."

Dick, skeptical, and Bud, confused, both returned to the mystery in the auditorium. Bud looked at the floor and back at Dick. Dick looked at the floor and back at Bud.

"Well?" he asked.

Bud stuck out his foot and kicked a piece of gum. It skidded across the floor and came to a stop at the end of the row. It looked like Bud had, indeed, scraped all the gum off the floor; what he had neglected to do was to pick it up afterwards.

Dick's mind was churning with disbelief, and his temper was welling up inside him. He turned to Bud, thinking of how to go about strangling him and getting away with it, and decided it was best if Bud wasn't anywhere near him today. He said,

"Just go home, Bud. Just go home for today, and when you get here tomorrow, pick up every piece of gum that you scraped off the floor in here. Just so that we are totally clear, after you pick it all up, throw it in the garbage can."

Dick stood shaking his head with his shoulders slumped in defeat, and he turned to walk away, leaving his aging employee standing by a theater chair.

"Okay" was all Bud said, and he quickly turned to leave before Dick could change his mind about giving him the remainder of the day off.

He was totally unaware that he had not completed his assignment to his boss's satisfaction. *And* he had the afternoon off. This was such a great job!

Dick was now faced with removing the gum from the concrete steps and sidewalk outside of the school. Clearly, Bud was not the man for *that* job. Maybe Matt was up to the task.

Matt was a custodian from another school on loan for the summer. He seemed to have no concept of time. He just showed up on his bike whenever the mood seemed to strike him. He arrived at 9:20 a.m. one morning, ready for his 9:00 a.m. shift. Dick handed him a scraper and sent him off, explaining that he was to scrape the gum, all the gum and nothing but the gum off the sidewalk. Not wanting to run into the same mistake he had encountered with Bud earlier, he went on to explain that he was to throw it away after it was loose.

Matt was about forty, lived with his folks, and rode a bike that was too small for him, but he seemed to understand the responsibility that was laid out before him, as well as the obstacles. Because he couldn't keep an eye on him from his office behind the kitchen, Dick decided to do some paperwork from a table in the cafeteria, where there were windows all around offering a view to the courtyard and patio outside where Matt was supposed to be working. This is what he observed as he watched his employee go about his task: Matt would sit cross-legged in front of a piece of gum; he would scrape until it came loose. Then without uncrossing his legs, he would stand up, unwinding his body like a corkscrew as he stood, walk over to the large garbage can on the other side of the patio, and drop the piece of gum into it. He would look in, making sure the gum found its way to the bottom of the receptacle, then turn and find another piece of gum, sit down cross-legged, and repeat the process. Over and over, he duplicated the same procedure, loosen the gum, pick it up, stand, cross to the garbage, throw it in, watch it, repeat.

A small crowd began to gather to watch the man work through the windows in the cafeteria. It was summer after all, and there was not an abundance of urgency in the work to be done, so everybody had a minute to loiter. As I watched, I inquired,

"Why doesn't he just move the can closer?"

"Probably too heavy" was the reply. The can was a large weighted model designed so that the kids could not easily move it.

"Do you want me to find him a bag?" I asked.

"No." Dick chuckled. "I want to see how long he does it before he figures it out."

"It makes my knees hurt just watching him sit and stand up like that," I observed.

Dick just nodded, smiling to himself. As it turned out, Matt never did figure it out. He finished cleaning the concrete in the courtyard that day, one piece of gum at a time to the amusement of the rest of the custodial staff. To the amusement of the rest of us, Matt didn't show up to work the next day. No surprise there.

However, there was still gum to be eliminated, and we were running out of custodians. This time, the gum removal fell to Pete Murray, our little custodian with Down syndrome. Dick handed Pete the scraper, which had now been in the hands of three different operators, and he got a bag for the gum pieces so that the last fiasco would not be duplicated. So after Bud and Matt had done battle against the gooey, ugly mess we call gum, it was now Pete's turn.

Pete had been our custodian for many years. He was thirty-eight years old and had suffered from the syndrome since birth. He stood just over four feet tall and was 135 pounds of stocky mischief. He was a sweet, sweet soul who had a devilish streak. Pete was usually happy-go-lucky and always stubborn. To put it simply, Pete was a hoot. He not only kept us laughing at his antics and personality, but he also kept us on our toes year round.

Pete was obsessed with *Star Trek*. He always insisted that you call him Admiral Murray and if you ever questioned a decision he made, you would have to answer to the district office, which was known to Pete as the Federation, not unlike the Mother Ship. The only person with more authority, at least in Pete's eyes, was Admiral Kirk, whom Pete idolized and insisted he had on speed dial in case he ever needed assistance, even though Pete didn't even own a phone.

Pete always worked hard. The thing he worked hardest at was getting out of work, and he could be very cunning, but he was eager to please and determined to do a good job. On this summer morning, he grumbled a little as he put on his outback-type safari hat with the flap that covered his ears and neck, and he strode resolutely outside into the summer heat. He stood looking down at the messy spots of gum that had been on the walks since September of last year. Then he walked around the perimeter of the area to spot all the gum that needed to be removed. After he found all there was to find, he seemed to make a decision on how to accomplish his task and quickly got to work.

As all of this was going on, there was a group of us who were meeting in the conference room, planning the calendar for the next school year as we always did the first week after school was out. We purchased some snacks, and we were settling in to work. We were making some real progress when we heard a strange chopping sound outside the window. When we investigated, we saw Pete with a chisel and hammer attacking the gum that he'd been assigned to remove from the sidewalk. Pete was a no-nonsense type of guy, and he didn't mess around with a simple razorblade scraper. No, Pete decided to start right off with a chisel and hammer. Not only removing the gum but some of the concrete as well.

He had the chisel to the ground, and he was swinging the hammer with all his might. As the hammer connected with the handle of the chisel, presumably the gum was supposed to pop free of the cement. This might have worked in the super cold winter time when the gum was frozen, but in the middle of the summer when the sidewalks were scalding, all that happened was the hot sticky gum stuck to the metal part of the tool, then it was impossible to get it off the end.

As Pete soon discovered that this wasn't working, so his plan changed. His new plan was that he just needed to hit it harder with the hammer. As we stood there watching, he took a colossal swing, and just as he made contact with the chisel's handle, a piece of concrete came loose and was flying straight for the window where we stood watching him. The group jumped back a little startled just like when you are sitting in box seats behind home plate at a baseball game and the batter fouls a ball straight back. Even though you know the net is there to catch the ball, your reflexes still kick in, and you jump to move out of the way. That's what it was like as we stood at the window seeing the rock heading our way.

Well, we hadn't even had a chance to react to that first incoming piece of concrete when he took another huge swing, and more concrete came loose, spraying the glass with a few more smaller pebbles, plus a couple of pretty large ones. The assistant principal immediately darted for the office door, and before we knew it, he was hurrying out the front door of the school toward the little guy who thought he was doing a very efficient job with the task at hand.

"Whoa, pump the brakes there, big guy!" Mr. Montgomery, the assistance principal, shouted as he confiscated the hammer and chisel before any more damage could be done.

He replaced the more destructive tools with the original gum scraper made just for the job. Pete was not pleased that his tools had been replace and watched as Mr. M left with the hammer and chisel to return them to the custodian's office. However, Pete took it in stride and went back to work while we all returned to our calendaring project.

A few minutes later, we looked out to check on Pete again, and to our surprise, once more he had the hammer and chisel. We hadn't even seen him leave his post, but somehow, he had left, retrieved the tools, and was back on the job. He was just about to start pounding away at the gum on the sidewalk once more when Mr. M hurried out, yet again, to take the instruments of destruction away from him.

Time went by. We worked steadily on the calendar, and Pete worked busily at the task at hand. The next thing we knew, he was pushing a big plastic garbage can around the sidewalk, presumably to pick up the gum he had scraped. He was already ahead of Matt. However, all of a sudden, to our horror, he reached down into the garbage can to pick something out. It was such a funny sight because the garbage can was up on wheels and was nearly as tall as Pete. It was horrific because when he reached over the rim and into the can, we all thought he was going to fall in headfirst and be stuck with his feet sticking out from the top, kicking furiously.

As we looked on, both astonished and amused, Pete came up from the bottom of the can unharmed with, you guessed it, the hammer and his chisel. Oh, for crying out loud! He'd found the tools and hidden them in the bottom of the garbage can to get them back outside undetected. Once again, we confiscated the tools, but this time, we put them right on the conference table where we were working so that even if he found them again, he would not be able to take them and use them on the unsuspecting concrete sidewalk.

A half an hour or so went by, and we were making some progress on the events for the next year when we heard a motor start up, and all of a sudden, a powerful stream of water hit the window with a loud crashing sound.

"That can't be good," someone in our group noted as we all rushed to the window, yet again, to see what the fountain of youth was going on.

Not to be discouraged from his task just because his hammer and chisel were gone, Pete had discarded the gum scraper and collected the power washer and a hose from the maintenance room in the back of the school. He was a crafty, stealthy rascal!

Pete, being the agent of chaos that he was, had wheeled the machine out to the front of the school, connected it to the hose bib, and was attempting to power spray all the pesky gum from the sidewalk, and apparently from the windows of the office as well. He'd seen Dick use the power washer before, and he'd been waiting for an opportunity to give it a go. He saw us all looking out and gave us a big smile and a friendly wave and tried his best to control the hose, which was clearly too powerful for his grip and was getting the best of him.

We all rushed outside to help Pete get control of the hose. After a few of us had been sprayed and power washed, we unhooked the machine and put the equipment away. It was getting close to lunch, and we all decided it was time for a little break. Pete needed a break from scraping gum, and we needed a break from Pete scraping gum, the project he had started that morning.

Pete always left at noon. He was the one custodian who only worked half a day. When he was ready to leave for the day, I walked out to praise him on the work that he had done that morning. He looked down at the gum that was still left and said, "Gooey."

"Yes," I agreed. "And ugly too," I added.

"My no like gum," he informed me, and I nodded in agreement.

"*G-U-M*," I spelled it out. "Gooey, ugly, messy," I concluded, and it was his turn to nod as he considered my words.

He knew full well that he would be doing this same task tomorrow morning, and I knew full well that he would be doing everything he could think of to get out of it, put it off or at least have a little fun with it, like using the power washer.

By the end of the summer, all the mounds of gum were gone from under the desktops and the feet of the science tables. The floors were free from the tacky pools of goo. All the gum had been scraped *and* picked up. Now, the walks were clean for the next wave of students to arrive in September, though they may have had a few more divots than usual.

CHAPTER 15

FOR PETE'S SAKE

There are a few days in middle school that are as traumatic for the students as picture day. One day in the spring and one in the fall, outfits must be just so every hair in place, teeth and braces brushed and shiny, and they must stay this way from the time the bus picks them up in the morning to bring them to school until the time their class is called down to the auditorium for their turn in front of the camera.

The only day that seems to cause more trauma than picture day itself is the day the pictures come back to the school. This day can be more upsetting than a lost cell phone, an ugly zit, or being unliked on Facebook. When school pictures come back less than picture-perfect, many tears are shed, and the office staff must pick up the remains from shattered dreams of pics that they hope will look somewhat like Angelina Jolie from Hollywood instead of looking exactly like Hannah Jones from Pineview Avenue.

Every year I heard hysterical comments like "My ponytail is so tight, I look like I'm bald!" "I look like I have a fro even though I kind of do." "My dimple is pointing out today, and it looks like a wart." My personal favorite: "I was talking to my crush right before they took my picture, and my face turned out all red."

We always encouraged the staff to have their pictures taken at this time for their inclusion in the yearbook. The teachers that refused to do this had the same picture in there year in and year out for ten, fifteen, or twenty years. Sometimes they were unrecognizable because the picture of them was so old. Other staff members looked forward every year to having their picture taken. One of these was Pete. In fact, Pete was always the first in line to have his photo snapped. He would wait patiently while the cameras were being readied and the fake scenes of autumn and spring backdrops were set up.

You might remember Pete from the earlier chapter regarding gum. He was one of our custodians and had been for nearly twenty years. He was born with Down syndrome, a genetic defect that struck him even before birth and made him like four hundred thousand other children in our country who suffer from the mental and physical deficiencies and challenges of the condition.

Pete was the only custodian who would be photographed and, in fact, loved it. He was happy in the spotlight, which he was, literally, for the few seconds he sat upright turning his head this way and that in front of the camera for his yearbook picture. Pete's Down syndrome may have altered him physically, from his short legs and arms to his distinctive facial features, but his personality was pleasing, trusting, and sincere. He had a wicked sense of humor, and despite a tongue impairment that made it hard for him to speak, he was outgoing and brave. His limited communication skills made it necessary for him to depend on the kindness of others, and most were kind and tolerant, although there were times when he sorely tried one's patience.

After one particularly stressful picture day, the office staff decided we all needed a soda, so off I went to the local C-store to fetch the refreshments. One Coke, one lemonade, one Dr. Pepper, and three Diet Cokes, and a package of cookies. As I was exiting the parking lot back toward the school, I could hear the stern words of Pete's mother in my head: "No extra treats for Pete!"

Mrs. Murray was Pete's mother, and she was a stickler about how much Pete ate. The problem with keeping treats from Pete was that Pete was always looking for them. He loved to eat and had an insatiable sweet tooth. Each fall, when the students and the office staff returned to school, everyone noticed that Pete had lost a few pounds over the summer. This is because his mother would put him on a strict diet for the summer and there were no "extra treats" available at the school for him to partake of. Once school started though, the treats would come rolling in. From registration day when the office personnel would provide a potluck lunch for the rest of the staff helping out to the first day of school when the principal would supply bagels and juice for everyone in the main office, there were always plenty of snacks to enjoy.

I would always try to obey Mrs. Murray's requests and go along with her restricting Pete's treat intake, mostly because she was not one to tangle with, but at the same time, it was always so hard to say no to Pete. I would say as much to Mrs. Murray.

"Okay," I protested, "but he can be pretty persuasive when he wants something."

"Yes", she'd agree, "and he can be sneaky when you tell him no, too, so you really have to watch him."

Oh, great. Not only do I have six hundred teenagers I have to watch but my custodian as well. Nonetheless, I did try to curb his brownie and Tootsie Roll consumption, difficult as it was.

Pete just loved to munch, and he knew just how to get the stuff he wanted. He would always eat breakfast with the special needs kids because he like to help take care of them and watch over them. He kind of "adopted" a few of them. We knew he would never to take anything off their trays, but he would wait until after they'd finished and left the cafeteria, then he would eat anything that was left over from their meals. So being the designated Pete-watcher, I had to work with the special education teachers to make sure everything was thrown away before they left the area.

He would also cruise through the office every morning just to see if maybe someone had brought in doughnuts or made cookies for the staff. Many times, there would be those extra little things for people to nibble on like popcorn or chips and salsa.

For Teacher Appreciation Day, we had a couple of dozen doughnuts on the counter behind the front desk. Since we only had four or five people that were housed in the office, we had many doughnuts leftover. Pete came nonchalantly walking through and asked with his big puppy eyes if he could have one. Risking a scolding by his mom if she found out, I said,

"Let's cut one in half, and we can split it." I suggested, and he was very excited at this prospect.

"Okay!" he said enthusiastically.

It was a busy morning with a lot going on, and I had seen Pete come through the office several times, and it occurred to me that I'd seen him come in two or three times, but I hadn't seen him leave once. I confess that I hadn't been keeping a close eye on him or the box of sweets. I saw him coming down the hall toward the office, and I quickly turned my attention to my computer to a phantom task. He was watching very closely, and I tried to not let on that I was watching him right back. He slipped into the office, sauntered past the counter, eyeing the doughnuts and enjoying their aroma, inhaling the sweet smell with a big smile on his face. Then very casually, he would pick up the plastic knife that I had used earlier to cut our glazed fritter in half and cut another pastry down the middle and grab one-half of it and keep going right on by. Then the little devil kept walking right behind my desk where he thought I wasn't watching and out the door at the back of the office.

For Pete's sake!

I wondered how many times he had done that this morning, and I silently prayed that Mrs. Murray never found out that number. It turned out that the task of overseeing Pete was akin to nailing Jell-O to the wall.

The one thing that she would allow him to have during the day was diet soda. He would treasure this, and he couldn't wait until he could take his break and enjoy an iced-cold drink. The thing that Pete loved the most was a Diet Coke from McDonald's. He knew that if he came into the office to ask, I would probably pop to the McDonald's on the corner just down from the school to pick up a Diet Coke for him, and one for myself, as well. He must have also figured that I would buy, because he never questioned how I got them or where the money came from. He always just knew that when I came back he would have a Diet Coke with extra ice.

All our custodians would carry walkie-talkies, and sometimes Pete would insist on carrying one of those to call me in the main office during the day. If he wasn't calling about one thing, he was calling about three more. Everything from where Dick, his supervisor, was to wanting to know when our next day off was going to be. When he was working particularly hard at getting out of a task, I would hear the radio crackle, and Pete would ask, "Pete to main office. Going to 'Donald's today?"

I would respond, "No, Pete, not today," or "Yes, Pete, would you like a Diet Coke?" depending on how crazy things were and if I could get away.

It got to be such a habit that I had to restrict these calls and the corresponding sojourns to once a week. Every Wednesday became Diet Coke day. It would give us both something to look forward to in the middle of the week, and it would keep him off the radio so we could get some work done.

A few times, when I first started working in the main office and Pete didn't know me very well, he would come in and try to bribe me to go to McDonald's for him. He would say,

"If you go to 'Donald's today, My will buy." Then he would hand me a gift card for McDonald's with $5 or $10 on it.

So off I would go, only to find out when I got there that the card was empty. I actually fell for this trick twice before I learned that whenever Pete said he would pay, it meant I better have some money with me because I was going to need it.

Aside from eating, the other thing that Pete loved was arguing with Bud, our other daytime custodian. Bud was a foot and a half taller than Pete and had twenty years on his smaller counterpart, but the two men fought like stepbrothers. Every year, Pete would try to goad Bud into retiring, because he thought once Bud was gone he would move up in the ranks of the custodial staff. Every year, Bud would find an excuse not to retire. Bud would enjoy teasing Pete, saying, "It's too much trouble to retire." Then follow up with, "I'm never going to retire."

Pete would turn red in the face and respond with, "You old! You need retire!" in a loud, exasperated voice.

For every excuse he had for staying on the job, Bud would have an excuse to not work while he was actually on the job. He would complain about his back or an old football injury. He would take the long way if he had to go to another wing in the school and stop to take a little break or two while en route. He would work an hour or two, then take a fifteen-minute break, then work another forty-five minutes to an hour and take another fifteen- or twenty-minute break. More often than not, when you saw Bud sitting in a random chair somewhere in the school, he was sound asleep with his chin on his chest, snoring loudly.

Bud would do half his job, and then he'd find Pete to bribe him with candy to do the other half, risking the wrath of Mrs. Murray. Usually, Pete would finish much quicker than Bud and do a more complete job. Pete would sit and figure out a problem that Bud had been struggling with for days, then he would never let the elder forget that he'd had conquered a leaky hose, clumping rock salt or pesky mop-bucket failure. Sometimes, Pete would get the upper hand, stealing Bud's garbage can, moving his broom, hiding his coffee cup, or taking his hat and running away with it. Anything and everything he could think of that would drive Bud crazy.

Pete would vacuum the carpet outside the office just as a meeting began and would continue with the noise for far longer than was needed or until the meeting was finished, probably waiting to see if there were any snacks left over when the meeting was done. Bud would continually pass by and tell Pete to stop vacuuming. Pete would just ignore him and keep cleaning the small patch of carpet. This would make Bud crazy, and Pete knew it, so it never ended.

Oftentimes, Bud would volunteer to go the McDonald's for a round of sodas for everyone. It was the one time that the office wasn't thirsty. Nobody trusted Bud to get drinks because every time he went, he got the order wrong. Oh, you wanted and unsweetened iced tea because you're diabetic? Well, here's a sweet tea you probably can't drink. Oh, you wanted Dr. Pepper with lots of ice? Here's a diet Dr. Pepper with no ice. Our principal would look at him and ask, "Bud, why would I order a soda pop with no ice?"

"I don't know," he'd say, "but here you go." He'd hand her the cup and walk away.

I'd swear that some of the animals in the biology wing had more sense than Bud. He would go to pick up a pre-ordered breakfast or lunch for the custodial staff, and nine times out of ten, something would be wrong. It's normal to have a few balls dropped now and again, but there was a lot of ball dropping going on with Bud.

"I swear I told them no onions," he'd say in a whiny voice worse than your teenage daughter.

I'd just shrug and shake my head and chalk it up to another mishandled task in a line of many and one more ball dropped along the way.

After a while, he wouldn't even suggest going for food or drinks. He started showing up to work with a two-liter bottle of pop to keep in the break-room fridge. Because he was watching his weight, or at least his wife was, it would always be the sugar-free variety. Of course, Pete would continually drink Bud's diet drinks. It was unclear if he didn't understand that the drink was brought by and meant for the older man or if he knew exactly what he was doing and it was just another way to drive Bud senseless with aggravation.

Pete would tease Bud mercilessly about sleeping and call him old and lazy. Because of this, many staff members, as well as teachers, would refer to Bud as Rip Van Winkle. Bud would get steamed and actually rise from his chair and leave the room when someone called him Rip, for short. Pete would laugh uncontrollably, then everyone else would laugh uncontrollably because Pete's mirth was contagious.

Pete was a people connector. He would bring us together. It was our goal with Pete to make sure that he was safe at work and happy. For Pete's sake, we would have to forbid him to run in the halls because when he ran, he would bend at the waist, point his head, and sprint like a missile, sometimes not stopping until he hit something or someone. He would throw his arms around you for a hug and bury his face in your chest.

He was frustratingly sweet, maddeningly funny, and infuriatingly manipulative, but our school would not have been the same without him, and it would have been a much drearier place without Pete around.

CHAPTER 16

SCHOOL LUNCH DISMISSED

O de to the school lunch lady:
   Don't worry if your job is small and your rewards are few. Remember that the mighty oak was once a nut like you.

School lunch. You might as well say institutionalized meal, airline cuisine, prison food, gruel from a Charles Dickens novel. It just doesn't make your mouth water or make your brain hunger for that next great culinary experience, does it?

Of course, we are talking about teenagers and specifically teenage boys who can have an afternoon snack that consists of all the leftover spaghetti from last night, half a chocolate cake, and a quart of milk and then ask, "What's for dinner?"

Most teenagers are perpetually hungry. The difference between the boys and girls is what they hunger for. The boys all want to look like the athletes they see on TV, and the girls all want to look like the models, thus they eat accordingly. However, boys and girls alike were all ravenous by the time lunch rolled around. So after long mornings of choir, band, or gym class, when the bell rang for lunch, it was literally a mad dash to the cafeteria.

We had a no-running policy in the hallways of our school and signs everywhere that read, "SPEED LIMIT: WALK." But come lunch time, those signs were all but invisible when it was a tidal wave of twelve- and thirteen-year-olds crashing down on the lunchroom with all due speed. The kids who brought their own lunch had a distinct

149

disadvantage in this area, because they had to go to their lockers to retrieve the lunch sack or box they brought to school before they could make their trek to the lunchroom.

"It just isn't fair," one girl complained. "The kids who bring their lunches should be able to go to lunch sooner than the kids who buy their lunch."

True, but when you took into account that the kids who bought lunch had to stand in line to wait, the home-lunched crowd actually ate much sooner. Besides that, who said life or lunch was fair?

The kids who ate school lunch were speedier to their destination and dashed as quickly as they could so that they would be at or near the beginning of the line. It was always the goal to be the first in line. There was just a carnal desire to beat everyone else even though there was always plenty of lunch to go around. It was like *The Great Race* without the huge pie fight or sometimes with the huge pie fight. You just never knew what was going to happen, because anything could.

We had lunch moms or monitors who would be in the hallways five or ten minutes early to get ready to try to stem the tide of human flesh in search of sustenance. These brave souls were volunteer mothers with children who attended our school. For a free school lunch, they would come to school for thirty-five minutes a day to oversee the chaos and pandemonium that was also known as lunchtime.

Every parent should have the opportunity to spend a few lunch hours with their teenagers in the school cafeteria; they might not even recognize their child. It is quite unlike dinner at home with the family. It could actually be very enlightening. These moms would show up at the school dressed in their best Abercrombie and Fitch, hair just done and makeup perfect, and put themselves directly between the hungry children and the nourishment they craved. At risk to life and limb, they would try to keep the kids from running in the halls toward lunch, and they would try to keep the cafeteria neat and the consummation of food orderly. Worthy goals, to be sure, but quite difficult tasks.

It never worked. Every day by the end of the period after the eating frenzy, they would come into the office with their hair disheveled, their blouses stained, and their ideals tarnished.

"This is impossible!" was the cry across the school grounds.

Herding cats seemed easy compared to managing hundreds of teenagers during lunch.

In 1946, President Harry S. Truman signed the national School Lunch Act, and the School Lunch Program was born. Across the nation, federally assisted meal programs sprang up in over one hundred thousand schools, and 7.1 million meals were served nationwide that year. By the end of 2011, over 200 billion school lunches had been served. Then in 2012 a change occurred. It wasn't just a subtle change barely noticed; it was a huge transformation that sent ripples over the mashed potatoes and gravy and shivers through a rainbow of gelatin.

Then First Lady Michelle Obama decided to make school lunch her signature issue. With the best of intentions in her heart, the only way to describe it was that it was, simply put, a disaster! Mrs. Obama set out to change all the established guidelines for school lunches to make them lower in sodium, sugar, and fat. This was not the worst idea since 20 percent of American children are or will become obese. The percentage of children with obesity in the United States has more than tripled since the 1970s. Today, about one in five school-aged children are considered overweight, thanks to the golden arches and Nintendo. So a change was definitely needed. Maybe not so drastic as to traumatize all school-aged children due to healthy eating. A modification was an ambitious goal, but I think she bit off a little more lunch than she could chew.

What she proposed astonished everyone. Virtually, all salt was to be removed from the food, and her new recommendations scaled way back on meat, protein, and anything with fat. It was her "war on obesity" in children; it turned out to be a war on our cafeteria food in general. Waste increased big time, and participation decreased noticeably. Lunchtime morale went right to the garbage disposal, literally. High school students were abandoning campuses during lunch to find something edible to eat. Even the teachers stopped buying lunch at school. It seemed that it wasn't worth the $2.85 they paid for it. There was not a Frito, Dorito, or Cheeto to be found.

The potato chips had gone the way of water in the desert. Teachers began keeping stashes of junk food in their desk drawers, hoping that there weren't any hungry mice in the building to find them. Everyone knew which teachers to go to if you needed a Hershey's kiss and which ones were good for Pringles. Pop prohibition took place across the district. Soda was banned from every campus from kindergarten to twelfth grade. Teachers were going through withdrawals. Cokes and Diet Cokes were smuggled into schools like so much contraband.

Michelle Obama instigated the first major changes in the school lunch program in fifteen years. Unfortunately for her, the schools, the parents and, most importantly, the students were not behind her. She was on her own. The basic lunches that the kids had come to know and love over their tenure in public school was about to be replaced with foods they wouldn't touch with a ten-foot spork. Everything that the kids actually liked was now gone or made into something healthier for them with more whole grains, no salt, and less sugar. Yikes!

The cause of one-third of American adults being obese happened because they grew up that way as children. Happy meals took the place of family meals. Fatty but cheap burgers and oil-drenched French fries became the dinner of choice for a big portion of American families. They became addicted to the sodium, and what's more, they came to love high-calorie meals being served on the corner at the drive-ups.

Most fifty-year-old adults with heart trouble and diabetes wouldn't eat the food we were serving in the cafeterias, let alone a growing thirteen-year-old with no health problems whatsoever. Many students across the nation began protesting the changes, arguing that it didn't matter how healthy you made the lunches if no one was going to eat them and they were just going to end up in the trash. Parents began protesting because their children now wanted to take lunch from home which is a pain in the patootie if you don't have time to fix a sack lunch for three or four kids every morning.

Headlines screamed, "STUDENTS DISMISS SCHOOL LUNCH" and "SCHOOL LUNCH: NO CAKE WALK."

Well, maybe not to that extreme, but the public was disgruntled, for sure.

Once the first lady's new program was put into effect, we were required to replace everything in our vending machines with items that listed whole grain as the first ingredient. This included chips, crackers, cookies, and even Kellogg's Pop-Tarts. If I were to tell you that the only Pop-Tart you could eat would have to be a whole-wheat Pop-Tart, would you still buy it? Me neither.

So we ended up removing all vending machines because the kids quit using them. She was correct in her view that the trend of raising obese children has to stop; however, a less cut-and-dried (literally) approach may have been better accepted by the nation's children and their parents.

Fruits and vegetables went from being canned peaches and French fries with a ketchup packet to small plastic containers filled with fresh grapes and cherry tomatoes. These were a big hit! Not because the kids ate them but because grapes and cherry tomatoes made great ammunition for the food fights that inevitably occur in a school lunchroom, *and* they came in handy carrying cases.

The standard hamburgers that the kids would eat if there wasn't anything else to their liking was changed to a soy burger on a whole wheat bun. Mrs. Obama, have you ever eaten a soy burger on a whole wheat bun? No one has! They are the driest food on the planet next to a whole grain Pop-Tart. And it doesn't matter how many ketchup packets you squeeze on either one, they are still dry. On the upside, the whole-wheat buns made excellent Frisbees and could go nearly the length of the cafeteria if your throwing technique was correct.

It was always fun to observe the excitement and disorder in the cafeteria at lunch, especially if you were watching from behind the glass doors of the office. It was like watching *The Hunger Games* on a life-sized television. Though it was always best to be behind the glass and away from the mayhem. If a food fight starts, and trust me, it doesn't take much, the last place you want to be is in the thick of it.

Navigating the shortest distance between two students who are throwing hand-trimmed stems of broccoli or sliced dill pickles at each other can be a big challenge. Not only do you have the immoveable mobile tables with eight stools attached, but you also have several hundred students hindering your advancement. Whether or not that was on purpose was always up for debate.

Not to mention you may actually be ducking the flying cherry tomatoes while enough brown rice to accommodate a large wedding party rains down on your head. You might also have to hurdle a soccer ball or two rolling across the floor. It made the compulsory death match in *The Hunger Games* look like a holiday weekend picnic.

A word to the wise: the faint of heart should not volunteer for lunchroom duty. It is definitely not for wimps. That being said, I *did* volunteer in the lunchroom for an entire year.

I know what you're thinking . . . "You just said *not* to do that."

You'd be right; however, word was spreading through the carpools about the perils of volunteering for lunchtime monitor duties, and we were losing so many non-gratis helpers that it fell to the administration to do lunchroom detail, and I wanted to help them out. So off to the trenches I went, unarmed and exposed to all manner of food stuffs, arguments, and jokes, but not unawares. I did know what I was getting into. I had to break up a few fights, separate more than a few couples necking, and some days, I did not make a lot of friends, but for the most part, the kids behaved. For the most part . . .

The first day that I worked the lunchroom, duty I forgot about the five-minute rule to be out in the halls and in position before the first lunch bell rang. So the kids got a pretty good head start on me. I saw them dashing from every hallway toward the cafeteria. They came from the north and south and from the second floor pouring down the stairway in front of the office into the lunchroom. It was comparable to the running of the bulls in Pamplona, Spain. I raced out of the doors from the carpeted office to the slick tile floors of the lunch area with my neatly ironed cotton dress and my high-heeled shoes. When I hit the newly polished floor, I skidded like an antelope with ice skates on a frozen pond. As I ran trying to keep my balance and trying not to look like a fool, I cried,

"Stop running, stop running! Slow down, stop running!"

But I was too late. No one would heed anything I was saying even if they could hear me, which clearly they couldn't because they didn't stop running. Although they did try to ignore me, they couldn't because of the spectacle I was making of myself skating around like I was on very thin ice in my heels. I was afraid that when I reached the students I would crash into them, and it would be like a bowling ball hitting the pins at the end of the alley. I finally came to a skidding stop at the head of the lunch line. I believe they call this a snowplow stop in hockey terms. I halted with the grace of a pregnant hippo, and to my credit, I avoided knocking anybody over while remaining upright myself.

It wasn't exactly like putting myself between Pooh Bear and his pot of honey, but it was close. It was more or less like being in the middle of a den of grizzlies after a kill. I slowly backed away and tried to not let them smell my fear. Eventually, they got used to my presence, and I felt safe being among them and mingling in their environment. Teenagers feel comfortable around their own kind, but throw an adult into the mix, and not many people would give the adult much of a chance to make it out with her pantyhose intact.

I witnessed a lot in my lunchroom experience, everything from holding hands and kissing to crying and praying.

I was supervising the cafeteria one day early in the school year, and I was patrolling the perimeter, trying to keep an eye on everyone at the same time, which is fantastic if you have twenty eyes and can maneuver them in such a way as to not miss anything important. I noticed Josh, a shy seventh grader, unwrapping his sandwich and chips. He was sitting alone at a table but talking to friends nearby. Distractedly, he picked up his apple and took a big bite. A look of total panic and alarm crossed his face, and he immediately dropped the apple like it was the most disgusting piece of fruit he had ever bitten into. As it rolled away from him across the table, he looked around to see if anyone had seen what happened. Well, I saw it; I just didn't know *what* I'd seen. I mean that apple looked perfectly sweet and crispy to me.

He quickly folded his hands on the table in front of him and bowed his head and said a quick prayer, blessing the remainder of his apple and his lunch. After he finished, everything was fine; the dismay was gone. He retrieved his apple, took another huge bite, and went right on laughing and joking with his friends. I am aware of the whole Church and State controversy in public education. There isn't supposed to be any prayer in school, but Josh's small blessing over his sack lunch was so sincere and cute it nearly brought a tear to my eyes. He just had to bless that meal before it was eaten, proving, to me at least, that prayer at mealtime was alive and well at this boy's dinner table. I was secretly hoping, if not praying, that he had included a small prayer for the lunchtime overseer, as well.

CHAPTER 17

SAVE THE CHEESE
BURGERS IN PARADISE

Back-to-school night. Four words that can strike joy in a parent's heart if they've had seven kids and this is the last one they will ever attend or excitement in a student's heart if they have now left behind the small world of elementary school and will now enter the six-classes-a-day world of junior high. For parents, back-to-school night meant summer days were over, keeping the kids entertained was done, and it was time for them to go, well, back to school.

Mothers all around the neighborhood and throughout the land rejoiced as September approached and their children would be in the company of the teachers for the next four months or so. They were so happy and giddy they would do anything to help with back-to-school night. They couldn't wait to accompany their children to the school for a night of meeting the teachers and finding their classrooms. "Won't that be fun!" moms would exclaim trying to convince the young teenagers that this year school was going to be so fun they would never want to leave.

In the words of American novelist and magazine editor Edgar W. Howe:

"If there were no schools to take the children away from home part of the time, the insane asylums would be filled with mothers."

For teachers and school staff, it was a whole different prospect. The following sums up the teachers prospective of back-to-school:

The summer holiday was over, and young Jack returned to school. Only two days, later his teacher phoned his mother to tell her that Jack was misbehaving. "Wait a minute," Mom said. "I had Jack with me for the last three months, and I never called you once when he misbehaved."

We tried so hard to make back-to-school night a fun and exciting event, not a chore to be dreaded by parents, teachers, or students. We tried to bring a carnival atmosphere to the occasion.

"A barbecue," we thought collectively. "Everyone loves a barbecue. This will be great!"

We were going to bring new meaning to back-to-school night. The entire community would be involved; it would be something they would look forward to every year. The whole district would be talking about it and singing our praises!

The first year we tried it, we held the event out on the patio attached to the side of the school. We deliberated, planned, schemed, and arranged everything down to the last balloon and mustard packet. We had it all—music, games, activities, and food (lots and lots of food). All the parents showed up, went to the classrooms, met the teachers, wandered around the school, then left. They didn't even come to the barbecue/carnival. You would have thought they'd at least come out to find out what the music was all about. Sadly, no, they really didn't care.

After standing in front of the grill all night, only a handful of parents came out to the patio to eat. *Oh well*, I thought, *my husband is an outdoor guy, and campfire smoke is like an aphrodisiac to him. And I definitely smelled like a campfire.*

So all the teachers and staff had dinner. We insisted they have not only a hamburger right of the grill but a couple of hot dogs too. Fresh fruit and cookies were handed out like sparklers on the Fourth of July. We made bags of goodies for all to take home, yet still we had an abundance of chow.

Afterward, we all sat despondently in the main office, wondering what happened. Did all those parents not know about the event? Did we neglect to market our fantastic concept, or did they just decide it was a dumb idea? Above all else, we were wondering, *What the Ronald McDonald were we going to do with all those leftover hamburgers?* They had been cooked three hours previous, and the ladies in the office were afraid they might not be good to eat.

"Nonsense!" Mr. Montgomery, our assistant principal, said. "I will take a few home tonight, and the rest we can put in the fridge in the break room and have for lunch tomorrow."

We all looked at each other warily. Finally, I said with all the enthusiasm I could muster,

"What a great plan! I'm excited to be a part of it!"

Finally, everyone agreed to save the burgers. After all, back-to-school night was over, and we now had to turn our attention to the morrow, the first day of school, and the rest of the school year—God willing it would go better than the carnival at back-to-school night.

The cleanup was over, and everyone left to go home. The next day came, and we were back to school for good. The year had begun, and everything was in full swing. The office was as chaotic as a chicken rodeo with a lot of running around and cackling going on. The eighteenth century political activist, Thomas Paine once said:

"The real man smiles in trouble, gathers strength from distress and grows brave in reflection." Clearly he never worked in the main office of a middle school. Brave reflection didn't really sum up the atmosphere in our office on this, the first day of school. There were the usual late stragglers that had forgotten to register their children for school, and I wondered, "How can you possibly forget *that?*"

But they did, and it was my job, along with our registrar and office clerks, to help them through the registration *and* parenting process. As we were solving the problems of the world one student at a time, someone noticed that we hadn't seen much of Mr. Montgomery that day.

"Has anyone seen him at all?" I asked, but no one had—at least no one admitted to having seen him.

At just that minute, he emerged from his office, looking a little green around the gills.

"Are you all right?" I asked him, worried about his appearance.

"Yes, just a bit of an upset stomach," he replied, "I think it might have been those hamburgers I ate last night."

"We suspected they might not be the best to eat after sitting out all afternoon." I stifled an impish smile and made a mental note not to feed the others we had saved to the staff for lunch that day.

"No," he continued. "I think they were fine, I just think I ate too many of them."

"Well, how many of them did you eat?" I asked, curious now as to the source of his tummy ache.

He looked up toward the heavens as if trying to recall the exact number of burgers he'd consumed.

"Four or five, maybe six" was the answer, but the plot thickened, and the mystery continued when he added, "And a couple of beers after I got home."

So was Mr. M not feeling perky because the burgers were bad, because he had too many of them, or was it the beers that finished him off? I was beginning to think that we may never know.

"I'll have some more for lunch today and see if those affect me the same way."

"You are going to eat more of them today?" Mrs. Graham asked incredulously.

"Of course," he said, like we should all just know and accept that. "It's the only way to know for sure why I'm sick."

We, the mothers and wives of the office, gave him the are-you-sure-you-want-to-do-that look. None of us could believe that he was actually going to eat those burgers again.

"No, you're not!" cried Ms. Graham. "I won't let you."

Then she got the yes-I-am-and-you-can't-stop-me-cause-you're-not-my-wife look, and the burgers came out again for lunch, but only for Mr. Montgomery.

Sure enough, after the second burger, the stomach gurgling began anew.

"It could still be from last night," Mr. M argued.

"It could be, but how far are you willing to go to find out?" I asked.

"I am going to have another one," he said defiantly. He was resolved to prove to us that his stomach, his constitution, and those blasted burgers were just fine. It was his will against ours. We wanted him to stop eating them, but he was bound and determined that those burgers were not going to go to waste.

After a few days of stomach cramps and waves of nausea, Mr. Montgomery was back to normal, and the burger debacle was over and done with, although a few of us were still snickering about it weeks later. To his credit, Mr. M did not miss a day of school and was right there laughing about it with us.

The next year we decided to not be as subtle in our marketing of the carnival/back-to-school night. We plastered flyers and banners everywhere. We mailed out back to school night carnival information before we even sent out registration pamphlets. Nothing was going to stop us from having the funnest food, the coolest carnival, and best back-to-school night ever, and everyone was going to know about it and show up and be happy to be there. Or so we thought.

We switched it up just a little so that we were no longer barbecuing on the patio between the building and the soccer field like the previous year. That year, we were going to trick people by putting the food right out in front of the school, right as they walked up to the school to enter the front door, the smell of barbecued burgers would hit their nostrils, and they would have to stop to see what was going on.

We still had balloons, music, and jugglers, the jugglers being the staff bringing out all the stuff for the dinner. Burgers, hotdogs, buns, chips, drinks, bottles of ketchup, mustard, and relish all were up in the air like so many bowling pins being juggled by experienced circus clowns. We were all set and ready to go. The office staff and all the teachers had been preparing all day, waiting to meet the new students for the coming year and their parents. Everything was just perfect, and then we heard it, thunder in the distance.

"It's not going to rain," insisted Mr. Montgomery. "It's the middle of August, and it's been over 90 degrees every day this week."

"You're right," someone said, and we all agreed; however, we still kept a cautious eye on the sky so we could evacuate inside should the showers start.

The evening came, and the event started, and people were eating and enjoying themselves. Mr. Montgomery and Mrs. Graham had on their aprons and were busily flipping hamburgers and turning hot dogs while I unwrapped the buns and doled-out chips and cookies. It looked like everything was going smoothly. Then the sprinkles started, and the rains came. Torrents of water gushed from the clouds above, and we soon discovered exactly how Noah felt at the beginning of the great flood.

"It's okay!" Mr. M shouted above the noise of giant raindrops hitting the tables, grills, and people. "It's only temporary!"

Mrs. Graham gave him an everything-is-not-okay look and then looked at me. We decided telepathically that we should start moving everything under an awning that was inadequately covering the front entrance of the school. We moved the tables with the rain-soaked paper coverings and tried to protect the buns, paper plates, napkins, and potato chips from getting wet. Water was dripping from the edges of the awning and cookies were ruined, not to mention hairdos and makeup. You might be wondering, *What was Mr. Montgomery doing?*

He was still standing at the grill, wearing his white apron, still flipping burgers, singing a chorus of Jimmy Buffett's "Cheeseburger in Paradise." Occasionally, he would wipe the drops of rain off his glasses so he could see, and he would try to coax parents who were running into the building for their tours to stop for dinner, but of course, he'd wasn't getting many takers.

Eventually, the unexpected summer storm stopped as suddenly as it had begun, and as usually happens, the sun came out, and the weather turned sultry and humid as the water evaporated from the sidewalks and the temperature soared again. To this day, Mr. M still insists there was no rain.

"It was only a sprinkle," he will claim. "Hardly any rain at all."

Everyone that was there remembers it differently.

Even worse than the rain was the fact that because of the storm, attendance at the event was pretty small and, again, we ended up with oodles of extra burgers. Everyone was already scheming to keep the leftovers away from Mr. M to avoid the stomach difficulties of the previous year.

However, it all ended well because our FACS teacher took all the remaining must-gos home to make chili and shared with everyone the next day. So the burgers were saved and so was Mr. Montgomery's digestive tract.

The best part of back-to-school was the anticipation of finding out what kind of students we were going to have, which translated into what kind of year we were going to have. Actually, we could find this out just by calling the feeder schools which fed our school with the students moving on from theirs. If it was going to be really bad, the sixth-grade teachers would often call the junior high principals and give warning, saying,

"Watch out for Tommy. He can really be a handful."

This was code for "You are going to have two tough years ahead until he moves on to high school." One year we had a call that went like this:

"Hey, how was your summer?"

"Oh, great. We took the kids to Disneyland for the fourteenth time. Guess what we saw—the same stuff that we did the first thirteen times."

"Awesome, do you have Tommy Johnson enrolled there this year?"

"Yes, he seems like a good kid."

"Oh, he is, but his mom . . ."

Then dead air, I mean crickets. I wasn't sure how to respond, I could only imagine what Tommy's mom was going to be like.

"Just rip the Band-Aid of and tell me," I said, wanting it straight and not sugarcoated.

"She's not really a helicopter mom. She's more like Black Hawk Down" was the reply. "She will choose Tommy's friends, do his assignments, come check the playground for safety, and probably make sure the hot lunch is not too hot for him to eat without her blowing on it."

Oh boy!

Most parents are protective of their kids; that's just the way of life. Some of the most powerful bonds in nature are between orangutan, polar bear, cheetah, African elephant, and emperor penguin mamas and their young. These animals teach their children survival skills like finding food and shelter and how to find mates.

The redback spider of Australia is one of the most protective moms in the animal kingdom. It is highly venomous and very protective of her young spiderlings using her strong silken web to keep them safe and fed until they can fend for themselves. Eventually, however, the young spiders do learn to fend for themselves.

One of the most protective of all mothers in the entire animal kingdom is the helicopter mom. These mothers, who have been known to crash summer camps, are usually described as overprotective, dominating, intrusive, and annoying. Although the phenomenon of the helicopter mom is usually found in the maternal parent of the human species, fathers have been known to practice the trend as well.

These hovering mothers and fathers of the millennial generation have become known as helicopter parents, a termed coined around 2000. Helicopter moms swoop in to rescue their children at the first sign of a jam, afraid to let them fall or fail. Not a bad trait, some might say. However, these kids can emerge from their childhoods lacking the most basic of skills—housekeeping, addressing, and mailing a letter, even job interviewing. I have known mothers that would accompany their adult child to a job interview, and I've known others who have called college professors to give excuses for late assignments.

Studies show that 30 percent of high school students, ninth to twelfth grade, report parents who intervene on their behalves regularly, especially when it comes to school, robbing them of their ability to initiate, grow, learn, gain self-esteem, and be productive members of society.

Whether it be a 2,126-word research paper or a haircut for the prom, mom is there to leap in, take over, and get it done right, leaving Junior unfulfilled. Will this young buck be able to fend for himself as he faces the perils of adolescence and adulthood? Tune in next week for Mutual of Omaha's *Growing Up Wild* when we explore young chimpanzees who take the car without permission and are never punished for refusing to share with their siblings.

Speaking of growing up wild, on the flip side of the helicopter mom, way on the other end of the spectrum is the parent who brought their child in to register for school with dirty clothes, bad breath, and just-out-of-bed hair two days *after* school had started and asked,

"When did school start?" As in what day, not what time.

They try to fill out paperwork and can't remember the date their child was born; the student had to answer the questions and fill in the blanks for them. As I came in on one child registering while her mom looked on helplessly, she was saying,

"It's Wi-Fi, Mom. It's not a question, it's a thing."

Her mom seemed happy and relieved to relinquish control to her daughter, and it looked as though it was not the first time she had done so.

These relinquishing parents are known as free-range parents raising what used to be called latchkey kids. They don't know how late their children are out, who they hang out with, or when they get home. When their children get into trouble, the parents seem helpless and don't know what do to besides yell. I actually had a mother scream at me and say,

"I guess it's *my* job to teach my kid responsibility. I thought that's what I sent him to school for."

Hey, lady, we are just *disguised* as responsible adults here! We don't actually practice that stuff.

PART FIVE

IN THE END

CHAPTER 18

THE WHEELS ON THE BUS GO ROUND AND ROUND

The way the school system is set up on our state, the district has its main headquarters where all the administration for the schools takes place. Governing from a safe distance, we like to say in the trenches.

The district then is divided up into elementary schools (kindergarten to sixth grade), middle schools (seventh and eighth grades), and high schools (ninth to twelfth grades). There are about 127 schools encompassed in the district region. Many of these schools refer to the district office as the Mother Ship, not unlike the mother ship in the movie *Independence Day*, where all the small ships are controlled by the main entity, without which they all would perish. This was a fair representation.

Others designated it the Evil Empire from *Star Wars*, where the controlling body was more than just one ship and there were considerably more than 127 smaller squadrons to regulate. The empire had its Jedi and its storm troopers. It had the dark side and the good guys, and it had the familiar struggles between the two. Hey, at least no one referred to it as the Death Star, not that we knew of anyway. Our school simply referred to the district office as the DO. It was a neutral and safe identifier.

Each department at the DO had its own trials and tribulations. The accounting department was fairly small. It was housed way down in the basement, and there wasn't a single office that had a single window. If anyone needs a window to look out of to see the green trees and the coffee shack across the street, it's an accountant, but they didn't have this luxury. There were five accountants for the district, all women. They were a little ragged around the edges, with some tension and impatience with the schools in their charge, and who could blame them being locked up all day long without a window?

However, I will say about our accountants that they seemed comfortable, if not ecstatic, about being cooped up altogether all day long in the basement. They were extremely competent even though tolerance was not their strong suit. They shared their toys and played well with others of their kind.

The accountable accountants came to our school to do an audit one winter, and we put them up in our conference room with many windows, a large table for them to work, and all the coffee they could drink. When I checked in on them a while later, they had all the window blinds closed so tight that the room replicated their office space in the district building basement. I was so sad they weren't enjoying the windows while they had them. You can take the accountants out of the basement, but you can't take the basement out of the accountants.

Human resources had their issues too. Let's just say that their department was not a well-oiled machine. In truth, it ran pretty rough. Applications for jobs were continually being lost. They would ask for résumés to be posted by 6:00 p.m. EST when our district was in the Central Time Zone, which means many applications for excellent candidates never made it into the hiring pool. The personnel in HR were not the friendliest beings, which I always thought was quite strange. Wouldn't you want your most outgoing and helpful people in the department that had so much contact with the public? They are your frontline; they should be the most approachable and welcoming of all the departments . . . just a thought.

Even the IT department had its own quirks and characters, or maybe the correct description would be quirky character. IT (information technology) monitors and maintains the monitors and machines to which they are connected. IT intelligently transformed guys from normal blue-collar workers to discomfited beings who configure computer systems and diagnose hardware and software faults. Infinitely talented souls with strange sense of humors who solve technical problems, as well as problems with the operators and the errors they cause. Like the accountants, the IT guys were comfortable with others of their kind—you know, computers.

None of these departments, however, quite compared to the transportation department. They housed the transportation personal and administration in their own building on the district office grounds. They didn't mingle with the personnel of the other departments in the big-boy offices; it could be that this was by design. Some said that it was to keep the buses from coming in and out of the parking lot all of the time; my personal theory was that they wanted to keep the bus drivers and those whom managed them away from every other person working at the DO.

My husband used to work in the transportation industry and used to always say,

"It's not that complicated. We are just moving freight."

The same idea applies to the transportation department in the school district. We are just moving students. It isn't brain surgery or rocket science. However, in the eighteen years I spent with the school district, the logistics of this concept was too overwhelming to ever master. They would try to turn it into rocket surgery every time.

The first day of any school year was always a difficult one. By and large, nothing ran smoothly. Students were apprehensive, teachers were a little high-strung, and Murphy's Law was in full effect. The variable that would invariably make matters worse was the transportation department.

I used to think that during the off months of summer, they would use that time to brush up on procedure, practice the routes (even if they didn't change them, which they usually did) and just work on making their department a little more . . . efficient and, well, just better. But that never happened. They generally used the first day of school as the trial run for new routes and to check on the timing of the drives and generally iron out all the kinks.

At our middle school, seventh grade day was the first day of school; only the seventh graders attended. This was to give them a chance to learn how to open lockers, locate their classrooms, find the cafeteria, and get all of the jitters out before they were thrown into the mix with the eighth graders. Junior high is unfamiliar territory and a little scary at first. They were no longer in elementary school; now they were in the land of locker combinations, showers in the gym locker room, seven class periods with several different teachers and actual seats in the auditorium instead of foam pads on the gym floor where the stage was tucked away. Not to mention that now they had regular-sized toilets and not the mini toilets of elementary school. The counter in the main office was now forty inches high instead of thirty; the tiny grade-school word was left behind. The last thing they needed, along with all that, was a bus issue.

One year, late in August, seventh grade day began with all commotion of a parking lot after an outdoor concert. Parents were dropping off while kids were riding bikes, scooters, and skateboards—all of them trying not to get run over. All the buses arrived on time; so far so good. Except one, of course. Six buses arrived at the school at 8:00 a.m. just in time for breakfast with the exception of bus number 300, which came at 8:50 a.m., five minutes *after* the first bell had rung. Upon calling transportation, the answer was simple, at least to them. They informed us, to our surprise, that we had requested that bus number 300 arrive at 8:50 a.m. on the first day of school.

The phones were ringing off their hooks because the bus was late. Parents were standing at the bus stops along the route with their children on their first day of seventh grade, waiting for a bus that frankly could be anywhere. They didn't know if a bus was even going to show up. Some students were waiting alone, unsure what was happening and wondering if they should just turn around and go home. It was frustrating, disorderly, and unnecessary trauma for those poor kids on their first day of school. It fell to me to call transportation. Hot dog!

"I have a lot of upset children and parents," I said after I had calmly explained the situation to the monotonous voice at the other end of the phone.

She responded to my story with, "Well, we had a request." What?

"Why would the school request that a bus arrive after school had already started?" you might ask, which is what I asked.

"Why would we request 90 percent of our buses be here on time and the last one arrive late?" I inquired, my blood pressure rising like a thermometer in the summer.

Her response to that was, "Well, all I can tell you is it wouldn't have happened without a request."

"Was it a written request? Did you receive a call a letter or an e-mail?" I asked, ready to set my sights on whoever made *that* mistake.

"Well . . ." Pause. "No," said Candy, the transportation secretary.

"Did you think to call the school to inquire as to why that bus was to be late?" I asked because I was sure that it had thrown their whole morning into upheaval as it had ours.

"No," she answered again, and that was it. There was no debating or arguing, no rhyme or reason. No apologies or assurances of any kind. Just *no*.

Now I can appreciate how busy, frazzled, and generally emotionally drained an employee in our transportation office might be after the first morning of school; however, I grabbed this opportunity to remind her that this busload of students and their parents had also experienced at pretty awful first day of school. I was hoping that she would commiserate with me just a little bit and offer some remorse for the incident and maybe some reassurance that it would be the last time, but there was none to come.

During this time, I was trying to figure out how to get to her through the phone to shake some sense into her. Probably a good thing I never worked that problem out; I am afraid that much harm could have come to her. After a long awkward pause as I was waiting for her to come up with some plausible explanation, she said, "We can only cross our fingers and hope that it doesn't happen again." She really did say that.

So we did. We all crossed our fingers. We hoped and prayed that the random person who placed this ill-advised request would never have the inclination to mess everything up again and that this particular problem would not *ever* happen again. In fact, it didn't happen again, but there were plenty of other odd, inexplicable events in its place regarding the school buses.

One particular bus driver kept complaining about the noise on his bus. Again, *rocket surgery!* Driving a full bus, which is sixty students, all teenagers, is most likely *not* going to be voted the quietest, least stressful, most tranquil job in the land. News flash! It's going to be noisy all the time, without exception.

This guy was in our office at least once a week with a complaint. Writing a student up for swearing or shrieking or doing something, fairly innocuous that was bugging him. Sometimes he would call the dispatcher, who would then call me to have one of the administrators meet him at the bus to escort a boisterous student into the school. It's pretty much a given that if you have a low tolerance for noise, yelling, singing, cussing and the occasional spit ball in the back of the head, middle school bus driver may not be the occupation for you.

It was always hard to keep bus drivers. I'm not sure what they thought they were getting into when they applied for the bus driver position, but for some reason, it wasn't the job they had imagined. We had a new driver, a middle-aged woman who started and was trained like everyone else (on the first day of school), and she had the same route for weeks. She drove from the yard, through the neighborhood, six stops along the way, eventually ending up at the school. The catch was that she got lost or took a wrong turn every day! The route never changed, the stops were all the same, and the school never moved, and still she struggled trying to find her way. Invariably she was late every day.

I think that more tardies were blamed on the bus being late than anything else. The funniest thing was when one kid would come in late and say, "I am late because the bus was late." Never mind that he was the only kid out of sixty on that bus who was late. I can't say that it was always the driver's fault when buses were tardy. However, I am pretty sure that it was his doing when a bus driver of six years decided to "mix it up" a little and began picking up stops in a different order each day.

The whole idea behind bus stops is so the students can know exactly when and where they will be picked up to come to school in the morning and dropped off to go home each afternoon. This system has worked in public transportation for hundreds of years—well, at least a few decades—and there seemed no reason to change it now.

Two cute little girls came to the office together, probably so they would not lose the courage to report that their bus driver was "going backward at the stops."

"What do you mean *going backward*?" I asked. "Is he backing up?"

"No," they replied in unison. I looked from one to the other.

They looked at each other as if they didn't know which one of them was going to spill the beans. One of them rallied her courage and said,

"He goes to the last stop first and the first stop last." She looked at her companion who nodded, swallowed hard, and added, "Then he does it backward the next day."

"Every day it's different." Again, in unison . . . and the wheels on the bus go round and round.

Not wanting to, yet knowing I had to, I again called my buddy Candy at the transportation office.

"It's hard enough for these kids to remember to do the same thing every day when things work the way they are supposed to," I began. "When the bus driver decides to mix things up for them, it's next to impossible."

She apologized over and over and kept repeating, "I wonder why he is doing that."

My answer was, "We'll just have to cross our fingers and hope it won't happen again."

She giggled and said, "I'll have the boss talk with him."

In the end, the problem got fixed, and then we waited for the next crazy thing to happen in transportation. We never had to wait very long.

There were many instances where I volunteered to be a chaperone on a bus to a sporting event or other district function. One of these times was a state basketball playoff game in a city well north of our location. All the teams from all over the state who made it to the playoffs would converge on this event center. As you can probably imagine, it was a madhouse in the area and a free-for-all in the parking lot. Buses would show up early, late, or even on the wrong day, and there would be no attendants to show them where to park or even point them in the right direction. All told, the drivers tried to be courteous and park sort of in the same direction and in order of their arrival, but there was always one . . . one who had to park over there instead of over here or had to park this way instead of that way because it would be easier for him or her to leave after the event.

Usually among bus drivers, it was "all for one and one for all," but with this guy, it was "all for one and one for all after I get mine." Of course, my students and I were on his bus. This driver was yelling at other drivers, belligerent about where he was going to park and which direction would be best for exiting. He was swearing up a storm and was not at all quiet about it. Everyone was going to know his plight and his plan to fix it by parking wherever he damned well wanted to.

Once the bus settled in the designated spot that he'd picked, we were finally able to debark from the bus. After riding for nearly ninety minutes, needless to say, we were all ready to get out of the bus to stretch not only our legs but also our outside voices. The second the bus came to a stop, the kids were on the move, running from the bus and screaming like their hair was on fire. Luckily, I was in the habit of giving them instructions for behaving themselves and reboarding before we reached our destination.

After they had all departed the vehicle, I warily met with the driver to find out how he wanted me to reach him when the game was close to being over and we were ready to return to the school. He gave me his cell number and said,

"I am just going to grab some pizza somewhere close around here. So I'll be ready any time you are." He happily informed me.

"Okay, great!" I said, encouraged that he was so easy to work with after the whole parking episode.

The game was so exciting. Our team won the state championship, and the kids were all kinds of wound up. Then the time came to actually contact the driver. It was good that we knew where the bus was parked, and as I walked there and hoped that all my kids were doing the same, I called the number the driver had supplied me with. I know this will shock you, but there was no answer. Not to panic! I texted him that we were ready to go back to school and that we were all on the way to the place the bus was parked. Still walking, I awaited his return text.

I weaved my way through the parking lot and ran into some of the kids that I knew I had ridden there with. We laughed and talked about the game as we made our way to our bus. We came around a long row of buses, looking for ours. Lo and behold, our driver wasn't there, *and neither was the bus*! I stopped short and looked around hastily. I told the kids to look for a bus that had our number, and they all reported back that they couldn't find it. I called the driver again. I called the school, no answer. I called transportation, no answer. I called the principal and told him the problem.

"He was just going to grab some pizza!" I exclaimed as I echoed his words with a panicky pitch to my voice.

I admit that I was perplexed about where the bus could have gone; I thought he was just going to walk to find his dinner.

"Calm down," Mr. Parker said. "We'll figure everything out."

Usually, those were my words to a distraught parent or anxious student teacher, and now I was hearing them from my boss. I must be losing it!

Many of the buses from other schools were loaded and began pulling out. Bus after bus left, and the parking lot began to empty. Soon we were the only group left, and there was not a big yellow bus in sight. As we waited, our principal got in touch with someone in transportation, and they sent another bus in our direction, but we were close to sixty miles away, so it was going to be a bit of a wait. I think Mr. Parker was ready to jump into a bus and drive it himself to pick us up, but transportation found a driver and an extra bus. *Thank goddess of transportation*, my inner voice said sarcastically.

Since we were the last team to play, we were done pretty late. We were stuck out in the lot until our rescue bus reached us. As we waited and waited, it got darker and darker. I could not imagine where in the transportation universe our driver and his bus had disappeared to. You would think with all the technology available we would be able to locate him or at least the bus he was driving. Seriously, there weren't that many places you could park a school bus, right? But he never showed up.

Once we were finally picked up, we were returned to our school none the worse for wear. The kids actually handled it better than their parents who'd been waiting all evening to pick them up. Though it was late and well after dark, the team had won, and we all sang the school song as soon as the building was in sight. Mr. Parker was there to greet us, and we all gave him a big cheer.

The field trip was mostly a success, and if you are wondering about the AWOL bus and its driver, he had indeed gone for pizza and apparently a beer or six. He had driven the bus to the pizza place and forgot all about his bus and about picking up the sixty kids and their chaperone he'd left at the area two hours or so before. So that day, the wheels on the bus stopped going round and round, and that bus driver no longer had a job.

CHAPTER 19

THE BEST-LAID PLANS

I once heard a student say,
"I like going to school. I like going home. It's the time in between I don't like."

Whether it's the day or the year, the concept is the same. It's fun and exciting to start, and it's good when it's over and time to go home, but the in-between stuff is pretty monotonous. Once the school year gets going, things become pretty routine. I would not say that any two days are the same, because they're not, but aside from the occasional bird flying through the window, light bulb breaking and falling from the rafters, or broken waterline flooding the brand-new gym floor, the days seem to have an ebb and flow that catches you and moves you along whether you want to go or not. So you might as well enjoy the ride. This is how it was for the office staff.

For the students, the days seemed the same, period to period, hour in, hour out. Each day offered the same classes, the same teachers, the same announcements and the same lunches. There were, of course, exceptions to the monotonous school days that were one big blur. These were few and far between, but when they came, they were a burst of flavor like a new stick of gum on the tongue. These were fire drill days and snow days.

The first rule of any drill, fire, lockdown, or earthquake is preparation. We in the main office strived to make each drill better than the one before, each fire drill evacuation faster, and each lockdown tighter. We spared no expense in devising and revising our plans. However, in the words of Robert Burns from the poem "To a Mouse":

> The best-laid schemes of mice and men often go awry
> And leave us naught but grief and pain for promised joy.

The best-laid plans for our means of escape due to a fire suffered the same fate. They often went awry no matter how carefully prepared, calculated, and arranged we tried to make them. Students during fire drills were always like little streams coming from the classrooms and then melding together into a quickly flowing river, picking up speed as it ran down to the ocean and joined with the waves to crash onto the shore, or in our case crashing onto the soccer field, where we were all supposed to meet in the case of a fire.

Everything was perfect on paper as it frequently tended to be, but then in practice, it seldom turned out the way we'd considered. Each classroom had a specific door that they were supposed to use to exit the building. Classrooms on the second floor had a precise plan of escape down an exact stairway, out an explicit door, around the building, and onto the soccer field. In theory, as we deliberated in the conference room, this worked to perfection. In hindsight, corralling waterfowl would probably have been easier. Who knew that teenagers could not and would not follow the simple directions outlined for their safety? In a word, *us!* We should have known. I mean, we worked, taught, and had hundreds of examples every day where they didn't follow directions. Certainly, this wasn't about to change, even if their lives depended on it.

Each teacher had a colored flag they were to use to escort their students safely from the building. So far so good, except when the drill happened, the teachers could never find said flag. Once the flag was found and the kids were lined up at the door, sort of, the teachers would then lead them down the path to safety. Unless of course the students sought a better path that they thought would lead them to safety quicker, because they were sure those people in the main office had no idea what they were doing.

Once everyone was outside, there was a specific route to follow around the building to the soccer field. If this was the case, why did we have children running around the building in every direction? Some going clockwise to the north, some going counterclockwise to the south, some not stopping at the soccer field at all, just kept running around and around in circles. The best-laid plans of principals and staff just went awry.

As soon as everyone was on the field, they were supposed to line up with teacher and flag at the head of the line at the edge of the field, and the line of kids should have been heading away from the teacher toward the other side of the field. As it turned out, it was more like the student section at a college football game after upsetting a rival team, then storming the field. There was no containing them and no organization at all. This wasn't the way it was drawn up in the conference room; it worked beautifully in there.

The firefighters who came in their big trucks with their stopwatches timed us while chaos reigned all around them. They tried not to laugh, but in the end, they lost that battle. Chuckling and shaking their head, they would say,

"We'll give it another go next month to see if we can shave a few minutes off your time."

So every month, we would have either an earthquake drill, lockdown drill, or fire drill. The kids treated them like the recesses they used to have in elementary school. Freedom from the classroom, a chance to stretch their legs and an opportunity to yell at the top of their lungs.

The one time that we actually had a real fire. The super-obnoxious alarm scared everything the kids had learned so far that day right out of them as only a fire alarm can, and everyone flew into action. The teachers dropped their books, leaped for their flags, and spurred the students into lines, then they led the way to the soccer field, where they moseyed around like grazing sheep waiting to be counted. The fire guys showed up, dressed in their gear and ready for a real fire; everything actually went pretty smoothly, save for one exception. After the students were safely outside and lined up in crooked columns across the field, the administrators and the fire chief looked in through the glass doors and saw someone wandering around the back of the cafeteria by the kitchen doors. Very suspicious.

Could it be someone had set the fire? Could it be he was still in the building? The brave fire chief headed back into the building while his crew were already there checking out the classrooms to find the source of the smoke. The chief found the mysterious wanderer who turned out to be a delivery man with a delivery of frozen waffles for the kitchen. He found an open door and just walked in, not noticing that everyone else was out on the soccer field, waiting for the building to burn down because, let's face it, isn't that what every student is hoping for during a fire drill?

The source of the fire was discovered. It was a pan smoldering on a burner left on HIGH. Some indistinguishable substance was fused to the bottom and rancid, black smoke was billowing from it. We were all safe, including the delivery man, and we were given the okay to go back into the building after an adventurous afternoon.

High school students are the epitome of "If opportunity doesn't knock, build a door." In other words, if an opportunity to sluff class does not present itself, pull the fire alarm and create one. You just need to be ready with an escape plan. In fact, just pull the alarm, the office staff has already planned the escape from the building. All you need to do is make it to your friend's car and you're off to IHOP for breakfast.

In this age of technology, this utopia of information and instant gratification, the middle and high school student is found in its natural habitat. The drama that social media causes among the teenage crowd is the exact kind of spine-tingling drama on which they thrive. As they run about talking and texting, texting and talking they are not unlike a school of fish that is impossible to control. Trying to catch one and make them put their device away is an exercise in frustration, as any adult trapped in the teenage world knows.

This phenomenon was never more apparent than the day of the "big winter storm." As winter approached in our community, the weathermen became more and more excited about it. After all, summer weather was boring—blue skies and sunshine every day—but winter, now that was something the weatherman could sink his teeth into. It seemed that every storm that was forecast was THE STORM OF THE CENTURY!

Our district always set aside the Friday before Memorial Day as a makeup snow day. In other words, if there was a huge storm and we had to cancel school for a day, we would have that Friday to make it up. If we went the entire winter without a school-closing storm, we would have that extra day off and get a four-day weekend in May. Whooo!

This little gem was always present throughout the winter. We would all watch the forecasts, not only to find out what to wear on a particular day but to see how hard and how much it would snow and to see if other schools would be closing. Just the prospect of a snow day was exciting. Of course, if there were more than three snowflakes, the kids thought that the school should be closed for a snow day. The district on the other hand reasoned that if there is any possible way you can make it to work or to school, you should.

We had experienced a good number of smaller storms with four to six inches of powder already, but the night before the huge storm that actually hit us, the weather forecast was for "just a few inches on the valley floor." Business as usual, but the cold February morning when we awoke, it was much more than just a few inches. It had snowed well over a foot and a half, and there was no sign of the flakeage letting up anytime soon. I watched the morning weather prediction for the remainder of the day and made the following comment to the forecaster: "If I were wrong as many times in my job as you are in yours, I would have been fired long ago."

He didn't respond, nor did he acknowledge that he'd been a bit off in his original estimate of how much snow we'd actually see that day.

The morning news showed tree limbs that had broken off into the streets, carports that had collapsed from the weight of too much snow, power lines were down, the morning commute was strewn with fender-benders, and my dogs were sure the end of the world was at hand.

I listened as I readied myself for work and heard announcements of closure after closure of schools around the area. I called my principal who lived farther away from the school than I did.

"It's crazy!" she exclaimed. "They already closed the school for my kids, but I haven't heard anything from the district about us yet."

"Okay," I said. "I will just meet you up there then." I looked at the dogs and said, "I guess you guys are on your own. I have to brave the elements and head to work."

They were none too happy about it, and neither was I.

Nevertheless, I jumped in my little 4WD Jeep, and I was off over the snow-filled streets and the frozen tundra. I saw accidents everywhere. Buses were stuck, and people were walking in snow up to their knees. The world was truly a winter wonderland, except it was nowhere near Christmas and close enough to spring that it just made everyone cranky.

"If ever there was a snow day," I said to myself, "this was it."

I finally walked through the doors of the school only twenty minutes late. The usual fifteen-minute trip had taken thirty-five, but I made it. Others weren't so lucky. Thirty seven of our forty teachers had called the office, wondering if school was really in session that day.

"Yup."

The district had made the decision that things just weren't bad enough to close the schools. Though they never actually said it, we all suspected that the extra day off in May had a bearing on the decision. It might be miserable, not to mention dangerous today, but we'd thank them in May.

The snow always brings out the worst in drivers and definitely adds a new and exciting dimension to traffic. All the drivers that never leave their warm homes like to venture out in the snow. I think it just makes them want to feel alive to endanger themselves and others.

The percentage of kids at school that day was larger than the percentage of teachers because most of them lived close and had walked. The kids that were bused were all no-shows because the buses didn't stand a chance. Some of them were stuck in the muck to wait out the cavalry while being pelted with snowballs from the kids at the bus stops. The winter storm had turned the city on its ear. So there we were, the few daring souls that had braved the weather for the sake of education and the kids whose parents had made them walk the gauntlet of snow to school.

Since there were not enough teachers to cover the classrooms, the plan was to have all the kids and teachers that were in attendance meet in the auditorium where we would put on a movie until we had things figured out. After minutes of arduous thinking, we decided that as teachers arrived late, we would break everyone into classes for the day. The students had a different plan.

They all gathered in the auditorium for what we hoped would be only forty-five minute to an hour, and they all promptly took out their cell phones to begin texting. They texted friends that were across the auditorium, they texted friends sitting right beside them, and they texted their parents.

Nearly 100 percent of the kids that had gotten out to bed, jumped into their winter clothes, and trudged to school were texting their moms, complaining that school was cancelled and they were just watching a movie.

"Come and get me!" was the universal cry.

The main office was flooded with calls. Even though we had power in our building, it was too bad that the snow hadn't taken out the phone lines. Twitter lit up, and we needed to take some of the adults from the auditorium to help us field calls in the office.

"Are you guys really closed?"

"Is the power really out?"

"Are all the teachers really absent?"

"Is my child okay?" one anxious mother asked. "He says there is panic in the school."

"Should I really drive all the way over there and pick him up?"

"Is school canceled, or isn't it?" another edgy mom implored. "I keep watching the news, but they say it's open, but my daughter is texting me that you are closed and no teachers are there."

The most frequently asked question, which I couldn't answer, was "Why didn't the district just cancel school today?"

Over and over again, I explained that we were indeed open and functioning, and "I know they probably should have, but here we are."

I tried to console all of them without actually saying their kids were lying through their braces when they said classes were canceled for the day. Now, remember, these are kids, and they are kids who were just robbed of a snow day. They would say or do anything to get the day off. I don't know what actual stories they were telling their parents; I do know that the former group was thrown into a fear-induced state of distress.

"All our teachers are either here or en route, and classes will be held as usual. We have power, and we are up and running."

I tried to reassure them, and I tried desperately to dissuade them from coming to the school to pick up their children. That would just add another dimension of chaos that this day didn't need. I wasn't sure the office staff that was there could endure it.

It didn't work. The end of the world as we knew it was happening, and these parents wanted to spend their last hours with the children that were, by all accounts, trying to trick them into a day off.

Mothers dressed like Eskimos and dads in parkas and Sorels paraded into the office to rescue their darlings from the perils of the winter day at school. They all might as well have the day off because we certainly weren't getting anything done here. Parents were not happy about their kids embellishing the truth so that they could go home for the day, but since they had already come all the way to the school, they just signed them out anyway.

As the day wore on and things finally calmed down, we ended up with about 40 percent of our students in class and 95 percent of our teachers, so classes were smaller than normal, and the day was fairly decent despite the morning fiasco. Mrs. Graham wanted to take every cell phone away from every kid in the building, but that would have opened another can of worms, and we were about full of worms as it was. The kids on the buses that never made it were all excused for the day, so their snow day worked out great. The only thing left now was the cleanup.

We didn't have a lot of snow shovels, but the few that were available were manned by anyone who could push one and was dressed for the weather. The superintendent over grounds showed up to see how we were fairing, and as he stood by his big truck with a mug of hot cocoa, watching all the staff shoveling their behinds off, our principal walked over to him, took the mug from his warm chubby fingers, and said,

"Time to go to work, Marvin."

With a surprised look on his face, he reluctantly took the shovel she held out to him and began the dig-out. That was our one and only huge storm of the winter. I guess we'd been lucky. We'd survived the storm of the century, and it hadn't even cost us our snow day. Looked like that four-day Memorial Day weekend would happen after all.

CHAPTER 20

OH, HOLIDAY BUSH . . .
OH, HOLIDAY BUSH

In this day and age, where multicultural sensitivity is at an all-time high and political correctness has reached epic levels, a preposterous question wandered through my mind. At what point does discrimination against discriminators become reverse discrimination? Just wondering.

Back in the 1960s, everyone and their dog was advocating for freedom of speech, freedom of the press, freedom to bear arms, free love, free rides, freedom, freedom, freedom. The very people clamoring for freedom of speech, demanding it then, are now denouncing freedom of speech in the form of political correctness.

Now those same people are proponents of political correctness, exclaiming, "Hey, you can't say that! You can't do that! You can't think that!"

Sir Winston Churchill got it right when he said, "Some people's idea of free speech is that they are free to say what they like, but if anyone says anything back, that's an outrage."

The truth is that political correctness threatens freedom of speech and, for that matter, freedom of the press. It limits rights protected by the First Amendment. In 2009 the Hate Crimes Prevention Act passed by the legislation criminalizes crimes committed because of perceived race, color, or religion. It also protects a wider class of victims based on gender, disability, sexual orientation, or gender identity. It made crimes deemed hate crimes or crimes of bias in nature illegal and subject to harsh penalties under the law, and rightfully so.

At the same time, this act made political correctness, control by fear. Not only are actions against protected individuals punishable more severely, but speech is limited as well due to the fear of being charged with a hate crime or labeled bigot, homophobe, or racist. Acts of violence against anyone should be strictly penalized, we all agree. Any act of violence against a person just because of who or what they are is abhorrent, and the punishment should also be harsh so as to deter it from happening again. The HCPA punishes acts, not thoughts, but speech is used against those charged to prove motive and guilt.

However, at the risk of getting splinters in my behind from the fence I am sitting atop, it is the proven action itself that should be punished and not the thought or words behind it, as cruel and ugly as they might be.

In our school, we enrolled many refugees from many different counties, including Syria, Bosnia, Somalia, and the Sudan among others. For a stretch of four years, we had two refugees that were twin brothers from Haiti in our school. Each in their own way, they were a handful and at times hard to deal with, but together, they were agents of chaos. They were banned from the middle school grounds for breaking windows and trying to enter the school at night. They were banned from the high school basketball games because they repeatedly tried to climb from the bleachers courtside to the closed balcony one story up. They were banned from the library for writing in the books and tearing out the pages.

Midway through my high school secretarial career, I was assigned to chaperone a bus to a playoff football game. The spirit buses, as they were called, were divided up by classrooms with a roster of who was to be on which bus. It was all very organized and well thought out. I waited outside my bus for the assigned classes to come down, and I began to check in the students slated to ride the bus. François and Pierre, our two twin brothers, got to the front of the line where I was standing and informed me that they wanted to ride on the bus I was in charge over.

"You can't," I told them, "because you two aren't supposed to be on this bus. Your class is assigned to that bus." I indicated their ride by pointing to the bus parked behind us.

"But all our friends are on this bus," Pierre argued. "Just let us on," François added.

"If I let you on this bus, I won't have enough seats for the kids who are supposed to be riding this bus, and you will be marked absent on your bus," I explained.

They tried to argue a bit longer, as teenagers often do, and I overcame every argument they made. As they turned, none too happy, to walk away, Pierre said,

"You are just a racist."

"Yeah," his brother echoed. "You're a racist."

Needless to say, I was taken aback. Because I would not let them break the rules again and I would not let them have their way, I was labeled a racist. I was not, at that time, nor am I now, a racist. Indeed, I try to be a shining example of fairness and justice in action and speech. That said, how was I supposed to respond to this false and ugly accusation?

I put the frustration of the insult behind me and said,

"Your class is on that bus, and that is where you will be riding." End of story.

But it continued to bother me. I was offended at being called a racist when these two boys knew nothing about me. I was only doing the job I was asked to do. Chaperoning, not segregating. No one had called them a nasty name, no one had beat or hit either of them, no one had spoken harshly or even raised a voice, yet the insult was quick and biting on their part.

If a teacher or staff member had said that to me, or made any kind of a similar remark, he or she would have probably been made available for a different position in another district. But since they were students, minority students and refugee students, the comment went without note.

Just because someone does not agree with you does not make them insensitive, wrong, or politically incorrect. And just because someone expects you to follow the same rules as everyone else, whether in school or in society, does not make you oppressed.

Ralph Waldo Emerson said it perfectly:

"Let me never fall into the vulgar mistake of dreaming that I am persecuted whenever I am contradicted."

Of course, no one wants persecution, bigotry, or cruelness in any way. We do not strive as a society to shower insults and hate upon our citizens. However, lively debate and difference of opinions not necessarily meant to offend nor be disrespectful is more likely than not perceived as bias or hateful. Those who stray from the politically correct or contradict what is popular risk being excluded, ostracized, and therefore, discriminated against themselves.

Enter political correctness, which has been labeled forced politeness. It's not necessarily correct, but it's sensitive. It is very important to be fair and kind to those who have been wronged, persecuted, or discriminated against in some way because of religious beliefs or skin color. But at what point does sensitivity become a deterrent to freedom of speech? When does political correctness turn into required or involuntary censorship?

Late in the 2016 NFL season, quarterback Colin Kaepernick took a knee during the national anthem to protest police brutality against African Americans. At the beginning of the 2017 schedule, more than just a spattering of players followed suit; entire teams were locking arms in solidarity collectively, not placing their hands over their hearts during the anthem.

"It's not about being disrespectful to the flag or the country," they claimed even though that's exactly what they were doing. "It's about shedding light on a problem in our society."

However, the only thing it shed light on was the NFL players and the brouhaha they were causing. The issue of police brutality that was the original cause for the protest went virtually unnoticed and unchanged by the weeks of protests taking place on the gridiron.

Sports like football have always been a cohesive force. They bring people together. Liberals and Conservatives alike root collectively for a singular team whether it's the Texans, Packers, or Patriots. However, in September 2017, sports and football became a dividing force to the country. Oh, and by the way, if you weren't on the same side of the fence as the protesting players, you were racist.

Some team owners were branded as racists because they publicly stated they didn't want their players kneeling during the anthem, and none of them would sign Mr. Kaepernick for millions of dollars to play football. President Trump was labeled a racist, *again*, because he felt the players should stand with their hands over their hearts for the anthem and tagged them SOBs for not doing so. Many believed the entire division of the country lay at President Trump's feet. Not the cops who were brutalizing as policemen and disrespected *all* law officers in general. No, the blame was squarely on the president and those who supported him. They were the troublemakers.

Local radio shows were broadcasting statements like,

"These boys need to have a platform where they can protest!" DJs were proclaiming.

I disagree. These boys already had platforms. Actually, they have the same platforms that I have—Facebook, Twitter, and Instagram some with thousands of followers. They and I could praise, protest, condemn, and/or write virtually whatever scatterbrained idea popped into our heads at any time. There was no need to take it onto a football field where it didn't belong in front of fans who made it very clear that they did not appreciate paying $250 per ticket to see it or be made a party to it.

I grew up a football fan in a house where Mom, Dad, and Grandpa were all avid fans. We all rooted for different teams and enjoyed healthy competitiveness. Despite that love, I boycotted football several weeks during the protesting until the players removed their demonstrations from the fields following pleas from the commissioner, the owners, and the president of the United States. Not a single person was asking them not too protest or limiting their freedom of thought or speech. We just didn't want to see it every Sunday, Monday, and sometimes Thursday nights in our living rooms. We tuned in to see the players we revered and respected play the game we loved. They had every right to protest, and they had the means to donate resources to help their cause directly. On the flip side of that, the owners had every right to not employ Mr. Kaepernick if they so chose; it did not make them bigots.

Then I started hearing stories from elementary schools in our district and districts in other states that fifth and sixth graders were refusing to put their hands over their hearts and would not recite the pledge of allegiance because they were protesting. They didn't know *what* they were protesting, but their favorite football players did it, and so by gosh and golly, they were going to do it to.

I have learned a few things during my time in public education since the turn of the century. I learned that kneeling during the national anthem is not unpatriotic. I learned that it's not okay to say "boys and girls," because a second grader that's not gender specific may be offended. It's not okay to dress up like a zombie or a caveman for Halloween because we wouldn't want to demoralize zombies or cavemen, and I learned that Christmas is offensive.

It was time to decorate for the upcoming holidays. We carefully chose decorations that would not bruise anyone's sense of self or sense of right and wrong. We laid out wreaths and bows and snowmen and sleds. Then someone decided that maybe we should call the district to find out if we could, in fact, have a Christmas tree.

"Yes," was the answer, "but . . ."

There was always a *but*.

"We suggest that you don't use colors associated with Christmas—like red, green, gold, or silver, and maybe not white, you know, just to be sure. You cannot call it a Christmas tree, and you most definitely *cannot* put any religious symbols on it, including, but not limited to, a star. Also, you really shouldn't send holiday cards to any district department that includes the word Christmas, and whatever you do, don't say 'ho, ho, ho.' That could really be taken the wrong way," the secretary on the other end of the phone stated.

Wow! It was like she had a cue card at the ready just waiting for someone to call and ask.

So we began the now not-so-much-fun-anymore task of setting up our artificial tree, with blue ornaments (our school color) and blue snowflakes (nothing too offensive there). Pictures of students and miniature ornaments of our mascot adorned our tree, and, oh yeah, *no star*. Then we gathered round and sang a rousing rendition of "Oh, holiday bush . . . Oh, holiday bush" and felt like idiots in doing so. This was too ridiculous; warm and fuzzy, it was not. What the devil were we doing and what the devil was the district and legislature thinking? There is not too much good you can say about a society where you can't say "Merry Christmas" to your coworkers without worrying that someone might overhear you and be offended, then brand you insensitive.

This politically correct thing was getting a little out of hand. I wanted to find out more about it nationwide, so I took to the internet, the source of all information and explanation. As it turns out, much of our society is affected in one way or another by politically correctness. Hiring for big corporations has been influenced, colleges and universities are impacted, and textbooks compromised. Petitions were proposed that would change what was in history books by omitting anything that might be construed as uncomfortable, distasteful, or politically incorrect.

No matter how bellicose, there were events and people in history that can't be erased even if they were unpopular, offensive, or politically incorrect. Nor should they be. It is ludicrous to revise textbooks to promote multiculturalism at the expense of teaching history as it actually occurred. You can't just rewrite history to improve it. It doesn't work that way.

"It is what it is," as all the kids in my school would say. "Shizzle the dizzle."

Christopher Columbus was a racist; we don't care if he discovered the Americas. We don't want our children learning about him. We shouldn't even have a federal holiday named after him. There shouldn't even be a university named after him, so our students will never know the insensitive mongrel who discovered the Americas. We can't have Martin Luther King Day because he was a womanizer, so we should have Civil Rights Day instead. Because no matter what good MLK brought to the world, he was a lecher, so no teaching about him. We don't want our children reading Shakespeare in school because he was labeled a racist, a sexist, *and* a classist, never mind that he was one of the greatest authors ever. Remove his books from the classroom and libraries? What's next, burning them?

There wouldn't be much to teach if we refused to teach the words of men or women who have been labeled politically incorrect at one time or another.

To wipe out racism, sexism, classism, lookism, and religious intolerance is discrimination in its purest form. Once all these *isms* are gone off the face of the earth, there are people who will find something else they don't like, and then that will be subject to impeachment.

The day will come when it's politically incorrect to eat glazed doughnuts in school if you don't offer chocolate doughnuts as well. Double-stuffed Oreos will be banned because they have more white cream filling than crisp dark cookie. Movies, music, ballets, and art will all need to be carefully scanned and censored or be subject to veto in the name of political correctness. Operas like *Aida*, *Othello*, and *The Geisha* are in danger of being shelved because they in some way promote injustice. Most operas created decades or centuries ago were written in a time where slavery was commonplace and women had virtually no worth. Was is right? No, but that's the way it was and that's how the script was written.

If you dig deep enough, you can uncover in every life a reason to call someone politically incorrect. Babe Ruth was often rumored to be racist even though he was a big proponent of the Negro Baseball League. Walt Disney was labeled racist because he produced "Song of the South." Elvis Presley was also tagged as racist even though he attended an African American church.

Simply put, freedom of speech today is not politically correct. Election debates are altered, football chants must be reformed, even cereal boxes have had to make changes due to racially insensitive artwork because a brown corn pop was depicted doing manual labor. In other words, free speech is fine unless it is deemed inappropriate, but who decides?

Back in the day, you know, when a cracker was just a crispy snack, if you did something stupid in school, someone would tell you, you did something stupid, and then you sat on a stool in the corner with a dunce cap on your head. "A bit overboard," some might acknowledge. "Unacceptable!" others might yell. Your grandpa would probably say after learning of the punishment, "Bet he won't throw snowballs at car windows again!"

Today, however, if you do something stupid in school, you just made a poor decision or a bad choice. You may have to visit in-school suspension during a lunch period, or if the decision was poor enough, a suspension from school for a day or two might follow. Accountability is a thing of the past, and a future of regulated thought and governed speech is in store for us as a country.

If a person does not accept an alternative lifestyle due to religious beliefs, they are labeled prude, homophobic, or backward, but doesn't the First Amendment give them the right to *believe what they want without repercussion*? Isn't that the whole premise behind political correctness?

Our first president, George Washington, once said,

"If the freedom of speech is taken away, then the dumb and silent we may be led, like sheep to slaughter."

Our contemporary society has made no clearly defined limitations on free speech; however, political correctness is the undercurrent slowly eroding it away.

More recently, Donald Trump, the forty-fifth president of our country, has been one of the biggest opponents of political correctness. He has been labeled a racist time and again for his inability and outright refusal to be politically correct. His words echo the same sentiment as George Washington's: "I think the big problem this country has is being politically correct. I've been challenged by so many people and I don't, frankly, have time for total political correctness. And to be honest with you, this country doesn't have time either."

He was labeled extreme, excessive, hated and offensive, but he wasn't afraid to say what he believed, right or wrong, and it may not have been what people expected from their president, but he had the freedom of speech behind him to do so.

CHAPTER 21

A HOUSE FELL ON HER SISTER

It was the last day of school! Yearbook signing, locker cleanout, teachers' talent show, and plenty of fun!

Yearbook signing was a time of reflection and tears. Tears because more often than not, a student's yearbook was on hold for a missing library book, and reflection over how that possibly happened because the student claimed they'd never checked out a library book in nine months of school. Locker cleanout was overflowing garbage cans and a pile of lost-and-found sweaters and coats long forgotten from the winter. And the teachers' talent show was always a blast because the only thing the teachers were good at was boring lectures and ill-timed pop quizzes. Right?

Arguably, the best part of the last school day was field day. It was a carnival of chaos, a gambit of games, a fiesta of unfettered folly that was looked forward to all year long. Suffice to say, P. T. Barnum would have been proud of the spectacle on the PE field. On this particular warm early June morning, the festivities were running high. Soccer balls were being kicked into the dunk tank, and dodgeballs were bouncing of buildings, fences, and heads and the noise level could be heard from the gymnasium to the street.

A simple throw of a Frisbee sent the whole shebang into disarray, more disarray than it already was on this lovely summer morning, the final day of school. Three boys were off on the edge of the school field, tossing a Frisbee as boys do, testing how high and how hard they could launch the circular disc. Larry, Joe, and Freddie, not unlike the three stooges, were having a wonderful albeit comedic time. It was a slightly windy day, and when one of them would throw the disc up, the wind would catch it, and they would all scramble to try to grasp it. It was a hilarious YouTube video just waiting to be viewed by millions. It all went south, however, when Larry wound up his arm and flung the disc skyward. Into the air it went, higher and higher. It began to come down to earth, then the wind grabbed it again and took it aloft. Suddenly, it took an abrupt nosedive and came to an unexpected stop when it hit the large branch of a tree just inside the school boundaries on the soccer field.

The three boys' antics also came to an end as they ceased their banshee-like screeching and stood at the base of the tree, staring up at the neon Frisbee caught in the branches of the crabapple tree. You may wonder, as I did many times, why, oh, why would someone plant a crabapple tree on the soccer field of a school? The answer is, who knows, but if I ever find out, I will have a conversation about how boys like to throw things, like crabapples, at anything that moves and even some things that don't.

Meanwhile, back to the Frisbee. After the wind had stolen the Frisbee and deposited it into the branches of the crabapple tree, the boys schemed among themselves the best way to free the toy from the branches of the awful tree. After all, it was late spring, and the branches were crowded with as many leaves as Mother Nature could fit onto a tree. Of course, they tried the throwing the dodgeball up at the prisoner to release it, which didn't work because none of them could throw it high enough. They then looked around for something long enough to knock it free from its perch, but it was no use. The Frisbee was hopelessly stuck. After arguing over the best course of action, the inevitable solution of climbing said tree was reached. What could possibly go wrong?

If your children are anything like mine were, they spent many a day hanging from the limbs of the big cypress tree in our front yard, swinging from the lower branches of the large tree while enjoying the cool shade, the fresh smell of the leaves, and the seclusion they provided. They also loved the view it afforded of the world from a different prospective. I would watch them climb from limb to limb and go higher and higher; their grins would widen with every new branch they reached, and you could see the sense of accomplishment on their faces.

I am sure that these three boys had felt that same feeling in the trees in their front yards, and I am sure that *they* were sure that they could climb that tree and free the Frisbee in no time at all. Larry, the heftier of the three, would boost Joe because he was the smallest— not the bravest but the smallest. Freddie was there strictly for moral support yelling,

"Come on, dude, you can do it!" To which Joe gave a doubtful look as he began to wriggle into the tree. The daring little "dude" made his way up the trunk of the tree, trying not to look down. He disappeared into the foliage of the branches and finally reached the branch that was holding the Frisbee hostage. He then shimmied out onto the limb, holding on for dear life while trying to appear brave and unabashed. His legs wrapped around the large tree limb and his arms reaching out, he made his way closer and closer to the object of this lunacy.

Finally, he reached it! He had it in his clutches and cried,

"I got it!" in a voice he hoped didn't sound too much like a frightened little girl.

He tossed the Frisbee down to his compatriots waiting below. His task completed, the young man was anxious to get out of the tree and back down to solid ground. That was where what could go wrong definitely went wrong. As he jounced and wiggled backward from whence he was, the boy flinched and stopped in mid-shimmy. Something was terribly wrong. A slow burning sensation was growing between his legs. A little slower now, he continued his descent, scraping the bare skin of his thighs along the bark of the tree.

After a long agonizing trek, he dropped to the ground, landed on both feet, and fell to his knees, clutching at his upper legs. He pulled his hands away to find them bloody. The bark had scraped a good part of the tender skin from the part of his legs that his shorts hadn't covered. It was here that an adult finally noticed the commotion near the edge of the field and literally came running to the rescue. However, it was also at that moment when a crowd began to gather around the scene.

It was then that I suspected the injured Joe was grateful that it was the last day of school. Had this incident happened on the first day of school, he would have spent the entirety of the year being teased and harassed to the brink of madness by the meaner kids in the school. After all, we were a school full of teenagers and we were not unfamiliar with the bullying element of the teenage psyche. In fact, we knew it all too well.

Bigger kids would hassle smaller, weaker kids, or cliques would give loners a hard time. We had our share of cyber bullying, ugly rumors, finger pointing, back stabbing, and best friends fighting on the bus during the ride to school then making up by lunchtime. The majority of the time it was kids being kids. But occasionally, we would have a serious issue that would require the intervention of the administration and/or counselors.

It seemed with social media on its side, the bullying problem was reaching epidemic proportions. Or maybe it was just because we now heard all about them. It was no longer swept under a big rug and brushed off as inconsequential. Bullying—more specifically, anti-bullying—became the catch phrase of the times. Movies were produced and songs sung shaming bullies, and anonymous phone numbers were set up to report the repulsive behavior. All this was undertaken to make people, especially kids, more aware of the bullying problem and its effects on those targeted by the harassment.

Another big problem that wasn't in the spotlight at the time, which was a problem at our school was bullying in the office place. As a matter of fact, it turns out it was a problem nationwide. I'd never really heard of workplace bullying or had a problem with it. I was quite naive until it happened to me.

The bully in our little corner of the world was a small little roustabout named Patty. She was four feet ten inches short, sporting shoulder-length flaming red hair. She was an ex-cheerleader with attitude to spare. When I first moved to the main office, Patty was considerably nice to me, overly nice, asking me questions about where I came from, what my family was like, how long I had been in the district, how I got that job, things of that nature. I thought she was quite personable. Yet as I came to watch her and know her better, my view changed considerably. I observed her throw tantrums with administration when she didn't get her way. I witnessed time and again her rude and abusive treatment of coworkers who had somehow crossed her path or wronged her in some manner. She was impolite to the parents whose children she didn't care for, and she would badmouth the principal at every opportunity. In her own time, that behavior was turned on me.

If I corrected her on any point the power struggle was on. We worked five feet from each other and rarely spoke. I'd ask a question and it would go unanswered. I couldn't get my mind around and had never understood such behavior. The most interesting part was when the administration decided to make a change in the main office and give Patty her own office. She came unglued. After they told her she was about to be moved, they hid in their offices, and her wrath was unleashed on the rest of us. Tears were shed, insults were hurled, and a temper tantrum that rivaled a three-year-old ensued.

In August 2016, *Forbes* magazine printed an article specifically about bullying in the workplace and the problems it can cause. The piece stated that 75 percent of workers in the United States are affected by some form of bullying in the workplace, isolating dedicated and productive employees, destroying office culture and morale and costing time and money. In June 2017, a WBI (Workplace Bullying Institute)—yes, it was a big enough problem that it had its own institute—US survey pinpointed 60.3 million workers have experienced workplace bullying or have been affected by it.

At first, I thought maybe Patty was just mad because a house fell on her sister, but she didn't have a sister, nor did she have a reason to be pissed off at the world. She had a nice family, her own home, a good job, cute dogs, but she was miserable at work and decided that if she was miserable, everyone around her should be as well. She would hassle, pester, frustrate, intimidate, and mistreat any one of the other secretaries that she found to be smarter, more efficient, prettier, taller, or higher in position than she was. If she didn't get what she set her sights on or if she felt threatened in anyway by any of us, look out!

She would stop at nothing to make everyone in the main office look bad. She would race everyone to answer the phone first. If someone walked into the office with a question, she would practically knock anyone out of the way to be the one to have the answer. At first, it was comical, but when her interference and sabotage became unbearable, it ceased being funny and started being infuriating. Intimidation was her modus operandi. She would raise her voice whenever possible, and she was quick to point out any mistake large or small.

Our office became like *The Wizard of Oz*. I was Dorothy, the meek and mild, and our cast of secretaries, both men and women, were lions, scarecrows and tin men. Our principal, Mr. Clark, was the wizard because he seemed to have all the answers to our problems, but in the end, he was powerless to solve them. All that was missing was Toto. Our students, of course, would be the munchkins. We all knew the role in witch Patty would be cast. She would throw everything at us as we traveled down our yellow-brick road—balls of fire, rusting rain, sleeping poppies, and the ever-popular flying monkeys.

Patty had many different jobs within the school, and she held every one of them hostage for ransom. If you were in her good graces or were her boss, things would go smoothly for you; if, however, you were an obstacle on her war path, whatever you needed would go straight to the bottom of the priority list. If she was mad at something or someone in the office and we would order something she was in charge of, she would go through all the drawers and cupboards to make sure that we actually needed that additional Styrofoam cup or extra yellow highlighter. She would keep track of everyone's breaks and lunches when we actually took them. She would take note of when we left, when we returned, and days that we were gone altogether.

She was fully aware of where each one of us would park so that she would know who was missing at work that day, then she would make it her business to find out the whys and wherefores of the missing employee. Patty would actually go out of her way to walk through every office on the main level to see who was present and accounted for and those who would go on her missing-in-action list for the day.

One day I parked behind the building instead of my designated spot, and she came marching into my office, looked up, and saw me behind my desk and stopped short, just staring at me as if in disbelief that I was actually at work and where I was supposed to be.

"I didn't see your car this morning," she stammered with a guilty flush coming over her face.

"Yeah, I parked in a different place today." I held her eyes with mine as she mulled this over.

"Well, why?" she asked in an accusing sort of way.

"Personal reasons," I replied, nice as could be.

"Well, I just thought you might be sick and wanted to find out if you were okay." Nice save, but I wasn't buying it.

"I am fine." I smiled. "Thanks for asking." I returned to my work.

The thing about Patty was the more you killed her with kindness, the more wicked she became. From that day on, she bad-mouthed me to anyone and everyone that would listen. She called me names that would make a truck driver blush. She quit talking to me altogether, which was a blessing in disguise. I swear it was like we were *in* high school and not just working at one. Unfortunately, she was also mean and cruel to the other secretaries in the main office, as well. And that would definitely *not do*!

My sweet coworker in the office was Cami and just about the nicest person on the planet, and Patty was even mean to her. Cami started having some health issues that we were convinced was due to the hostile working environment at work. She wasn't sleeping at night and was always worrying about what Patty was going to do. I began dreading work, which wasn't like me. I always enjoyed going to work and being with friends and colleagues, but it didn't feel like that anymore. Now I came into work and hopped on the Flying Monkey Airlines and made a nonstop flight every day over the rainbow where the stewardess was snippy, ornery, and cranky. Though I try to make light of it, the situation was becoming intolerable.

I can hear you asking yourselves,

"Did the principal know what was going on? Why wasn't any action taken against the unruly pain in the butt?"

The answer would be

"Yes. He did know." But as I stated earlier, he was powerless to do anything about it.

"I need documentation" was his plea time and again.

One thing I will give Patty credit for is that she was good at her job. She was efficient, well organized, and if in the proper frame of mind, she performed her tasks in a timely manner. It was only when her mood soured that things got really bad. Like most bullies, Patty had a Jekyll and Hyde personality. She could be warm and friendly if she wanted to be one minute and a four-foot brute the next.

So when we tried to document her behavior it seemed that we were the ones who were petty and vindictive. I felt so foolish writing down *Patty answered the phone faster than I.* Or *Patty gave unauthorized medication to a student that she wasn't supposed to. And she recruited office aides to drive students home who were ill during school.* I wasn't a tattletale by nature; I just wanted to have a pleasant day at work occasionally. The more we complained about Patty, the more determined she was to make life at work a living nightmare. It was time to do something, but what?

When investigating workplace bullying, its causes and its consequences, several stats jumped out at me. When asked by the US WBI, "What made the bullying stop?" 48 percent of the victims surveyed answered that they were forced out or just quit their jobs altogether to get away. Comparatively, only 26 percent of the people who were doing the tormenting were punished, terminated, or quit. So those were my choices—try to get Patty fired or quit myself. Because my head was beginning to hurt from banging it against a brick wall when it came to Patty, I opted for the later. A principal's secretary job came open in the district at another school. I guess I should have been cast as the cowardly lion. I closed my eyes, clicked my heels together three times, and I was gone. I left the job that I loved, the school I was loyal to, and the friends I'd grown to treasure behind me. I left my buddy Patty in the dust behind my ruby slippers and began anew.

As for Patty, you would have thought that with the person she disliked most in her workplace out of the picture she might have mellowed a bit. Nope. By all accounts, after I'd left, her antics and bad behavior continued on and are still present today. If you are a student and you are reading these pages, be a buddy, not a bully! If you are an adult and practice bullying as part of your daily routine, *stop it*. Grow up, learn to play, and work well with others and share your toys. We all have to here, so why not make it pleasant?

CHAPTER 22

THE FINAL DAYS

For students, the best day of school is the final day of school. It's the end of hall passes, tardy slips, homework, study hall and counselors. For the high schoolers, it means graduation parties, diplomas, and looking forward to college, trade school, or the job waiting for them at their uncle's construction company or their aunt's salon. For the younger crowd in junior high, the last day of school means field day, live music, and pandemonium. The teachers have mixed feelings about the last day of school. On one hand, it's their last day of classes for eighty-one days; on the other, it's field day, which by all accounts and testimonies can be a nightmarish complete with sticky snow cones and messy sunscreen.

Teachers didn't have it all that bad on field day. They mostly had to help keep the kids organized. On paper, it was a pretty simple task; in real life, a disaster waiting to happen. They all pretended that they were on board.

"This is going to be way better than last year," they would say while their fingers were crossed behind their backs.

When it actually came down to it, they would bring their lawn chairs, straw hats, and umbrellas and sit back to watch the bedlam unfold. In the office, the feeling was like when you're sitting in a chair with four legs and you lean back on two and almost fall backward, but then you catch yourself in the nick of time. That was the feeling in the main office on the final day of school.

The ones who really suffered on field day were the PTA moms. They were in charge of the whole field day experience. They planned the tug-of-war out of it. They organized everything right down to the color of the matching aprons the PTA moms would wear. The PTA moms started in April every year, meticulously planning and organizing a field day that was fun, safe, and predictable. The problem was it couldn't be both safe and fun because, let's face it, uproar is fun, meticulously organized isn't. Standing in line, going from station to station is, well, boing.

The cute PTA moms would have ten to twelve activities laid out in stations, which were things like ring toss, beanbag throw, trampoline, kickball, and the like. Then there would be the cool things—stuff like a waterslide, dunking booth, grilled hot dogs, snow cones, and cotton candy. The idea was that each class was given a station where the day would begin. They would line up and go through that station for twenty minutes, then a bell would sound, and they would rotate to the next station and so on. At first, they would line up, and they were about as patient as news reporters at a press conference.

The kids lined up at their first assigned station, just as planned. They would do the activity until the first bell sounded, then pandemonium would break out. Students would take off running in all directions, racing to get into lines for the most popular activities. The line for the dunking booth was around the building because who doesn't want to dunk the vice principal as many times as possible. Organization was lost, and panic ensued. Beanbags were thrown at everything except the targets. Ring-toss rings ended up around wrists, ankles, and necks if the heads were small enough. Mr. Montgomery was in the dunk tank; Mrs. Graham was trying to calm the PTA moms who were collectively losing their minds trying to get everyone in line, literally and figuratively.

"Sorry, ladies, that ship has already sailed. There will be no more organization today."

The kids' favorite thing about field day was when the neighborhood fire truck would come over to the school and spray water on all the students on the soccer field. Once the water hit the teenagers, that's when the clothes started coming off. Boys would bare skinny hairless chests, and girls with swimwear "secretly" hidden under their clothes would bare tankinis and halter tops. The PTA moms would be spinning in circles, biting their nails, pacing holes in their sandals, seemingly ready to pass out.

Mercifully, field day came to an end. Nerves were frazzled, Alka-Seltzer fizzed, aspirin tablets were gobbled, and we were never so ready for summer. Thank goodness it was the last day of school and students were dismissed early. The buses picked kids up at 1:20 p.m., and the exhausted PTA moms left with their children soon afterward. The final day was over. All that was left to be done was the retirement celebration for the teachers and staff that would not be returning the next year.

For most, the golden years come a little quicker than expected, and maybe it's a little rougher than anticipated, but most of the people I know that have retired have started counting down the days several months prior to the event.

"How long until you're done, Mary?"

"One hundred eleven days and about seven hours."

Retirement was always a bittersweet occasion. It is hard saying goodbye to seeing our friends and colleagues every day, but on the flip side, there is the pleasure of not awakening to alarm clocks at the crack of dawn, drinking a quart of too-hot coffee to jump start the brain, or having students step on your toes while trying to break up an argument over who is the better basketball player, Michael Jordan or LeBron James. Happy yet sad. Excited yet apprehensive. Years in coming, but here all at once, at least for public education careers.

I have said goodbye to many teachers over the years. Some were excellent instructors as well as compassionate caregivers. Others probably should have retired years before. I have said goodbye to staff members that are still my close friends today and to others that broke every rule in the book and still held on to their jobs to the end. Each goodbye was a new beginning with a new person, but all were teary, nostalgic, and touching. When I attended district events and knew far fewer people, I knew my retirement was getting closer. All the new teachers looked younger and younger, and I felt older and older.

As my friends neared the end of their careers, I was saying good-bye to more of my coworkers in the education world. It occurred to me that I would like to do something special for them as they left. Something that they could look back on with a smile and remember with fondness—something they would never be able to forget even in the worst cases of senility.

So I wrote a song for them that we would sing as a group of unfortunates who remained behind as those brave teachers we loved rode off gloriously to the golden years of retirement.

The name of the song was "AARP," and it was sung to the tune of "YMCA" by the Village People. Instead of making the *Y, M, C,* and *A* gestures with our hands and bodies, we substituted *A*s, *R*s, and *P*s. If you don't think a bunch of veteran teachers, as well as some new recruits singing and doing all of the awkward gestures to "YMCA" or "AARP" doesn't beat all, then you are not yet ready to retire. I guess I have truly seen it all after that.

Below are the words to the retirement version of "YMCA":

AARP
Old guy! Leave your classroom behind.
Think of all the hobbies you'll find.
So what if you're totally blind,
You can barely see your future!

Go out! Have a night on the town.
Screw it! Turn your hearing aid down.
Who cares, if you can't hear a sound?
You will finally be retired.

You belong to the *A-A-R-P*
It's fun to be in the *A-A-R-P*
Your friends are all there
with their walkers and chairs
You can all have wheelchair races!

You belong to the *A-A-R-P*
It's fun to be in the *A-A-R-P*
Get some insurance
while you drink your Ensure
You won't even need your dentures!

Can't chew? You can drink all your meals.
Jell-O shots have a whole new appeal.
Senior discounts! Are those things really real?
You can really save some money!

Sleep in! You can watch soaps all day.
Think of all the golf you will play.
Students are a whole world away.
There will be no need to hurry.

You belong to the *A-A-R-P*
It's fun to be in the *A-A-R-P*
No more students or grades.
No more parent tirades.
You won't have to check your e-mail.

You belong to the *A-A-R-P*
It's fun to be in the *A-A-R-P*
A new card you'll get
So you'll never forget
You can show it to your family!

Wake up! You'll get out in the sun.
Get up! But just walk, please don't run.
Hip replacement, they're just not that much fun.
Maybe you should take it easy!

Over fifty! Shingles may be in store.
No more will you face testing scores.
Colonoscopy? You just walk through this door
We will take some pictures for you!

You belong to the *A-A-R-P*
It's fun to be in the *A-A-R-P*
Assistance galore
You can travel and more
They even have their own magazine

A-A-R-P
I want to join the *A-A-R-P*

In my public-school career, I have seen veteran, seasoned teachers who plastered their classrooms with college football paraphernalia and dyed their hair bright red on game days, and I have seen a fresh green teacher bring a paring knife to work in their lunch bag only to have it wind up in a student's hand during a skirmish in the hallway.

I have known a home economics teacher who made all her own clothes from gingham and rickrack. I've known a family and consumer sciences teacher who set a fire in her kitchen while the shop teacher was teaching fire safety in the classroom next door, and I've seen parents cry and throw tantrums over school uniforms; far worse than their kids!

Yes, teaching has changed remarkably in the eighteen years that I have worked in the school system, and learning has increased exponentially. Elementary children now know more about computers that their stay-at-home moms who barely made it through PASCAL computer language classes in college fifteen years earlier.

Classrooms have changed from green chalkboards with dusty erasers to voice-operated Elmos. Textbooks have leaped from six-hundred-paged cumbersome hardbounds to handheld digital tablets. I have witnessed the Dewey decimal library system go from old-fashioned card catalogs with tens of thousands of cards to online files that hold trillions of megabytes of information, and I've seen testing transformed from a no. 2 pencil and bubble score sheet to online computerized exams. Research has evolved from encyclopedias to Wikipedia, and communication has progressed from a simple rotary telephone to complex digital platforms, thanks to the social media revolution.

Learning has followed suit. This technological era has expanded education in many, many ways. Rural students are learning the same material the same way that big city students learn, using digital learning tools and handheld devices. This hadn't always been the case, but now computers were enhancing study halls. Technology increases course offerings and resources and supports 24/7 learning to all students of every age.

Across the country, online schools with required and supplemental courses are available for virtual learning; newer, improved digital platforms link parents, teachers, and students to better accommodate essential requirements for grade advancement and escalate graduation rates. Oregon, Utah, Michigan, Florida, and High Tech High in California are only few of these online and open-school alternatives. Graduation rates have increased every year since the turn of the twenty-first century. In 2000, the rate for students graduating in the United States was 68 percent. It increased to 70.6 percent in 2005 and to 74.7 percent in 2010 dropping out of school seemed an option to some highschoolers. In 2016 the USA graduation rate jumped to 83 percent. President Barack Obama unequivocally stated, "Failure is not an option." imploring high school seniors to stay in school and graduate and they seemed to be listening. Students were not only learning more at a faster rate, but fewer students were dropping out of school. Technology was making learning more of a hands-on experience and a more exciting one. Making it more enjoyable than just listening to a teacher lecture in front of the class. Now far more students were graduating and turning their sites to higher education whether it be universities, colleges or trade schools.

The changes in teaching and learning have been years in the making, but there has been nothing subtle about it. They have been drastic and perpetual. As long as there are schools, there will be teachers, real or holograms, and there will still be students sleeping in class whether at a desk or in front of a computer screen, and there will still be the main office, the administration, the staff and the secretaries behind the scenes holding it all together.

ABOUT THE AUTHOR

C rystal has worked over sixteen years in public education, start-ing as a part-time library assistant and working her way up to principal's secretary. She has collected and complied many funny and captivating stories about school life during her career. She sees the humor in life and embraces the impossibility and absurdity in every situation, allowing her to work with hundreds of teenagers every day and still be sane enough to write about her experiences. Although she is no longer with the Utah school district, where she spent the major-ity of her career, she is still involved with the schools and teachers she loves. She now lives in Salt Lake City, where she was born, with her loving husband, Jeff, and her feisty dogs, Jeter and Jazzie.

CPSIA information can be obtained
at www.ICGtesting.com
Printed in the USA
FSHW01n0623221018
53194FS

9 781642 988505